NEXT BEST THING

CUBS FOR RENT #2

CHARITY PARKERSON

--Warning: This book is intended for readers over the age of 18.

INTRODUCTION

When artless meets masterful, it's a battle of opposites attract. The prize is a lifetime of happiness.

Orion is caustic and bitter. He doesn't like people, nor does he enjoy their company. There's nothing Orion needs beyond a good book. But Tucker keeps coming around and Orion doesn't understand why he doesn't want it to stop. As one owner of Cubs for Rent—a male escort service—Tucker already has too many men chasing him. Orion has no intention of joining the flock. Life doesn't care what he wants.

When Tucker met Orion, Orion accused him of being a liar and shut him down on every level. For someone who's used to getting any man he wants, Orion is an irresistible challenge. He's awkward and cranky. His head is always in the clouds and Tucker wants Orion with every fiber of his being. But this might be the one time Tucker doesn't get his way.

Orion has already suffered enough heartaches in his life, but Orion wants Tucker. That's a truth he can't shake. For once, Orion might have to set aside his books and live. How terrifying.

ONE

ORION MOON WAS ALWAYS unkempt and cranky. He gave zero fucks about his appearance. His dark hair always stood on end—like he didn't own a comb. He had eyes so light in coloration they looked otherworldly. If he had ever been attracted to a man or woman, Tucker had never seen it. The only time Orion seemed the least bit happy was when he had a book in his hand. Even then, Orion always had a deep line between his eyebrows, as if he doubted everything he read. Orion was also Tucker's best friend. Tucker couldn't stay away.

"Why do you make me do these things?" Orion bitched as he chased after the baseball he had failed to catch for the tenth time.

Tucker waited patiently for Orion to get the ball

and toss it back. He easily snagged it from the air as it came sailing his way. "It's called exercise and vitamin D. You need both. It's not healthy to sit inside all day, reading."

Orion shot him an annoyed look as the ball flew past him. This time, he didn't even bother trying to catch it. He simply went after it like they were playing fetch rather than catch.

Tucker shook his head. "You know you're an adult, right? Anytime I call, you can tell me no when I ask you to do things."

"Cool," Orion said, tossing back the ball. "I want to go home."

"No." Tucker swallowed a chuckle at Orion's annoyed expression. "You spend too much time at home. What does it hurt to entertain me for a while? I'm your friend. You're supposed to like doing things with me."

Orion growled. "Why do we always have to do things I suck at?"

"You don't suck at this, but I can find other ways to entertain you if you're bored." Tucker didn't hold back an ounce of innuendo. He always looked for any opening to flirt with Orion. Not only was it fun, but goddamn. Tucker wanted him. Plus, Orion kept showing up. No matter how much he bitched and complained about everything they did together, Orion still came by almost every day after work, as long as Tucker didn't have a date. Being one owner of Cubs for Rent, a rent a date service, meant Tucker had to be somewhat free to go out. Orion still hadn't admitted they were more than friends, so it was all good.

"I'm half tempted to fuck you. I couldn't embarrass myself any worse doing that than I am now."

Tucker took it in the gut. Orion had no idea how badly he wanted that. Still, he shrugged, trying to hide how much he truly wanted a guy who didn't see him in the same light. This was new territory for Tucker. He wasn't used to being the one doing the chasing. He tossed the ball again, watching as Orion went after it. "I could stay facedown while you're fucking me. That way, if you blushed, I'd never see it."

To Tucker's surprise, Orion's expression turned wicked. His mouth lifted slightly in the corners into a knowing smile—like he had a secret Tucker would kill to know. Tucker's brain short-circuited. He froze. His eyes refused to budge from the sight of that sexy grin. Tucker's body went on high alert. He had never wanted anything more than he wanted to hear

Orion's thoughts in that moment. Tucker was transfixed, so much so that Orion tossed the ball and clocked Tucker directly in the forehead. Tucker went down. He hit the ground, holding his head and wincing against the unexpected pain.

Orion rushed to Tucker's side and dropped to his knees. "Oh my god. I'm so sorry. Let me see. What do you need me to do? Do I need to call an ambulance?"

Tucker rocked and groaned. "Quick. I need you to kiss it. That's the only way I'll survive."

For half a heartbeat, Orion went completely silent, before he punched Tucker in the ribs. "Why do you always have to be so stupid? I thought I'd really hurt you."

Tucker rubbed his ribs, fighting back a laugh as Orion dropped to the ground beside him. Tucker snagged his waist and dragged him closer until Orion's head rested on his shoulder. "I can't believe you're refusing to treat my injury after trying to take off my head. Plus, you hit me. You hit a man who was already down. You're a cruel dude."

Orion turned his head and eyed Tucker's face. Tucker held his breath as Orion's eerily light gray eyes focused on where the ball hit. Orion was so goddamn beautiful. He left Tucker speechless sometimes.

Obviously finding nothing wrong, Orion settled down in his hold and turned his gaze to the sky. "You have to leave for work soon."

Without thought, Tucker dragged his fingertips down the back of Orion's arm. He didn't want to leave. Right here, with Orion, that's where Tucker craved being twenty-four hours a day. It didn't matter Orion only saw him as a friend. He was Tucker's best friend. Four months ago, when he had shown up on Tucker's doorstep, looking for Tucker's brother, Tanner, Tucker never expected he would even have this much with Orion. He was so armor plated that Tucker didn't know how to break through his shell. All he knew was, he couldn't give up. This man was the only one he wanted.

"Let me come over after."

Orion's gaze shifted back to his. "You know where I keep the spare key. I won't look for you."

He thought Tucker would find a bed partner for the night and wouldn't show. Tucker didn't know why Orion was so blind—why he couldn't see Tucker wanted him and only him. All Tucker knew to do was keep showing up until he wore him down.

Even Tucker didn't have a good reason for Orion to keep him. He just hoped Orion would.

As much as Orion enjoyed his spot in Tucker's arms, he understood everyone needed to work. He rolled to his feet and reached out to help Tucker to his. Orion fully recognized it was more for show. There was no way he could support Tucker's weight. Tucker would never point that out though. He was too nice. Sometimes, Orion wondered what it must be like to be so perfect. He couldn't imagine being so flawless that people fought to date him to the point of paying him just to be in his company. Orion wasn't jealous or resentful of Tucker for doing what he did. First off, they were just friends and he had no right. Secondly, he completely understood. Orion knew what it was like to be lonely and long for company. He really knew what it was like to crave Tucker. If he could afford it, and if Tucker didn't willingly spend time with him, Orion might be tempted to pay him too.

Once Tucker was on his feet, he didn't let go of Orion's hand. "I'll walk you to your car."

Orion knew he could wrestle his hand back, but

he didn't want to. He had to steal his touches where he could. With a nod, Orion fell into step beside Tucker. The walk to his car was much shorter than Orion liked. He hated these moment—when he had to say goodbye again.

With a sigh, Orion leaned against his driver's side door. Tucker dropped Orion's hand but moved closer. His body blocked any hint of a breeze, making Orion hot. At least, that's what Orion told himself. He refused to acknowledge his overheated state might have anything to do with the rampant lust coursing through his veins. Tucker ran both hands through Orion's hair. No doubt he left it standing on end. A sexy smile touched Tucker's lips as he stared at Orion's head and whatever mess he had made.

"It's like it's impossible for you to look bad," Tucker muttered, obviously talking to himself. His gaze dropped to Orion's. "Promise to miss me."

"You're never gone long enough for me to miss you."

Tucker shrugged. "What can I say? I love to bowl."

He was so dumb. Tucker never tried to make sense. Orion snorted out a laugh. "What the hell does bowling have to do with anything?"

With a delicious sounding chuckle, Tucker kissed his forehead. "You're right up my alley."

A loud groan escaped Orion. "You're the corniest person I've ever met." Orion's mouth said one thing, but he had never been more grateful for a stupid joke. It distracted him from the way his body immediately reacted to having Tucker's lips against his skin.

"Say you'll wait up for me because you know I'll be there."

Without thought, Orion gripped Tucker's t-shirt. It was like his hands had a mind of their own. "Some of us have to work during the day." Even to his ears, Orion's words sounded breathless rather than admonishing.

Tucker pressed his lips to Orion's forehead again. Instead of moving away, he spoke against Orion's skin. "You don't have to work tomorrow, but I get what you're saying. If you fall asleep, I'll just crawl in bed with you. I suggest you wait up unless you want me hogging all the covers."

Damn. Tucker had no idea how much Orion wanted that. "Fine. I'll stay up and wait. You're such a child."

Tucker's low and deep rumble of laughter

vibrated against Orion's forehead. "Whatever it takes to have my way. Love you. Be careful going home."

Orion dragged Tucker's scent into his lungs. Tucker's love was what a friend felt for a friend. Orion would take it. That was all he was likely to ever have. Orion recognized he wasn't soft or particularly lovable. He knew he wasn't the type of guy anyone was looking for. In truth, Orion had no idea why Tucker wanted to spend time with him at all. Whatever kept him calling, Orion needed more.

"Love you too."

Orion wished Tucker understood how much he meant it. No one else had ever gotten so deep. Most likely, no one else ever would. But Tucker had, and now Orion couldn't shake him. It was one hell of a predicament he had gotten himself into with Tucker. Orion had no desire to get out. He was such a mess.

TWO

TUCKER: *Oh my god. So, I'm at this event, pulling double duty, keeping a client company and to keep an eye on this guy who has been making some of our employees uncomfortable. Anyhow, this dude is tickling people. For real, tickling people. Who the fuck does that? He's like an octopus. You might say he has ten tickles.*

Orion: ***groans***

Tucker snorted as he read Orion's text. He covered his mouth and nose, trying to smother the sound. Tucker loved hitting Orion with bad puns. He hoped he made Orion smile. His phone buzzed again. Tucker checked it on the sly. He didn't want his date to catch him and get upset. After all, he was getting paid to be here. It would be beyond rude to text another man on their date, business arrangement or not.

Orion: *It sounds like he's just an immature old goat. He's a silly billy.*

A bark of laughter exploded from Tucker. Several heads turned his way. He bit his lip, trying to stifle the sound. He was at a silent auction and making an ass of himself, but damn. Tucker was bored. He wanted to get back to Orion.

"Would you like to find something else to do?" Kevin asked, leaning his way.

Fuck. Tucker scrambled to find a way to fix things. He quickly opened one of the funny memes on his phone and touched his lips to Kevin's ear. "Sorry. I got a notification on my phone. I worried it might be important. Turns out it was a notification from one of the ridiculous apps I follow." He flashed the meme Kevin's way. Tucker had no idea which meme he chose, but if it was saved to his phone, then it was something he had found hilarious.

Kevin glanced at his phone and released a bark of laughter that perfectly matched Tucker's earlier reaction. He breathed a sigh of relief as several heads turned their way again. Job or not, Tucker would never purposely hurt anyone he joined for dates. He completely understood the mentality behind hiring someone for the night. Sometimes, it was hard to be alone. More than once, he had wondered if Kevin hired him so he could hide from a broken heart. The man always looked sad. Not to mention, he was sexy, rich, and couldn't be more than thirty-five. His dark hair had a hint of curl at the ends and his eyes were a gorgeous shade of brown that always caught the light. There was no need for Kevin to hire anyone to spend time with him. But he did, and Tucker needed to respect that. Not to mention, Kevin was a big cuddly bear. Tucker didn't have the heart to hurt him.

Kevin stood and motioned for Tucker to follow. "Let's go and find something better to do. These people are boring the life from me."

Tucker tried hard to hide his relief. There was nowhere he would rather be than with Orion, but for now, he was Kevin's date. He was grateful for the chance to be anywhere else.

ORION STARED AT HIS PHONE. EVEN THOUGH HE knew Tucker wouldn't risk texting him again, he always had a hard time letting go of the snippets he got of Tucker's attention. Orion chewed his bottom lip when he realized he was smiling like a maniac. Tucker was just such an addiction. He made Orion laugh. No one understood how gut wrenchingly desirable happiness could be, until they didn't have it. Without Tucker, Orion didn't have it.

He leaned back in his recliner, pressed his phone to his chest, and closed his eyes. Orion could picture Tucker's body down to the finest details. He was gorgeous, and big. So fucking big. Wide-chested with massive arms, Tucker looked like a damn bull. Orion felt fragile and tiny, but safe when Tucker was around. Tucker always smiled and laughed. He was ridiculous and funny. Orion sucked in a deep breath. His cock stirred. Sometimes, at the most unexpected moments, Orion would find Tucker in his space, and he would think—for the briefest moment—Tucker was about to make a move. Then, the moment would pass, and Tucker was the goofball again. If Tucker had the slightest idea how Orion stroked himself with Tucker's name on his lips, Orion wouldn't be able to look Tucker in the eye again. The guy absolutely made Orion burn.

A wave of exhaustion washed over Orion. He had stayed up until two hours before he needed to be up for work, reading. He should have taken a vacation day today rather than waiting to do so tomorrow. Orion had known it was dumb, but he really felt it now that he had promised to wait up for Tucker tonight. A hint of sadness wormed its way into Orion's thoughts. It was possible he was staying up for nothing. Tucker didn't owe him anything. Whoever hired Tucker tonight might end up being the one to finally sweep him off his feet. After all, it had already happened to Tucker's brother, Tanner. Tanner had met his husband because of the brothers' business, Cubs for Rent. While Orion recognized that not everything the guys did were actual dates, since they sometimes did repair jobs or kept an eye on their employees at events, Orion knew any date—real or not—could lead to more. All it took was the right person, sweeping him away. Orion had nothing to offer but friendship, and Orion wasn't very good at that either.

A jaw-cracking yawn escaped Orion. Tucker's smiling face grew larger in his mind. Damn, Tucker was warm and comfy. Orion wished he was there.

ORION'S NEIGHBORHOOD WAS A QUIET, MIDDLE-class area not that far from Tucker. Late at night, like tonight, coming from home, it only took about seven minutes to get from his place to Orion's. Of course, he was usually speeding, but still. Orion's house was an adorable place with yellow siding and a perfectly manicured lawn. His flowers always looked amazing. The funny thing was, Tucker had never seen Orion do an ounce of lawn care. He assumed he paid someone else to take care of it. Orion was always one step away from hissing like a vampire any time Tucker made him step outside. Tucker smiled at the thought as he let himself inside.

The house was silent as Tucker came through the door. Of course, Orion's house was always quiet. While Orion owned a TV, it was only a small one in his bedroom. Otherwise, Orion's house was devoid of unnecessary sound. It was just another thing Tucker found appealing about Orion. Tucker didn't like noise. Too much busyness left him feeling agitated. He wasn't sure why Orion preferred the silence. For Tucker, it was because he had been raised off the grid by a psychotic father who beat him daily until... Well, it didn't matter. Tucker was grown now. His dad was dead. They had inherited his money. Hell was behind him.

Tucker made his way to the den. Orion rarely spent a minute anywhere else. Being surrounded by his massive collection of books made Orion happy.

Tucker had to admit, the room filled with mismatched bookcases and overflowing books smelled delicious—like dreams and old paper. He spotted Orion immediately. With his phone resting on his chest, Orion slept peacefully. There were dark smudges beneath his eyes. A hint of guilt sneaked in. Tucker had been keeping the guy up late and busy for over four months. No doubt the guy was exhausted. Tucker should leave him in peace.

For a moment, Tucker chewed on his bottom lip and stared at Orion. If he stayed put, his neck would be fucked up by morning. Tucker moved slowly, easing to the side of Orion's recliner. He snagged Orion's phone and plugged it in to charge. With that out of the way, he killed the lamp. He rushed to the bedroom and turned down the covers before returning for Orion. As softly and slowly as possible, Tucker slipped his arms beneath Orion and pulled him to his chest. Orion immediately snuggled closer. Tucker held his breath. When Orion didn't wake, he lifted the man into his arms and headed for the bedroom. As he set Orion on the bed, Orion stirred. Tucker froze. Orion grabbed his arm and hauled it across him—like pulling a blanket over him. Tucker slid in beside him. He was right on the edge and was one wrong move away from landing on the floor.

Then, Orion rolled, taking Tucker's arm with him, and Tucker found Orion's ass pressed against his cock. He was stuck. Orion's body molded against him and had him locked in place every bit as much as chains. Tucker settled in. He was here for the foreseeable future. As long as Orion stayed in his arms, Tucker would stay put. After all, it was possible this was as much as he would ever get of Orion's love.

THREE

FIRST, Orion blinked at his bedroom ceiling, trying to decide how in the hell he had ended up in bed. Then, he spent a minute staring at his bedside clock, wondering if he had lost power in the middle of the night. There was no way in hell it was two in the afternoon. Otherwise, he had slept like the dead, or someone who had partied all night. Next, a solid warmth beside him moved, sending his heart racing into his throat. Orion slowly rolled, praying he wasn't about to die. Tucker's huge body filled the bed, taking up too much space. Orion couldn't even blink. His eyes refused to give up their feast. He had no clue why Tucker was in his bed, but Orion had no complaints. He looked so peaceful. Orion fought a smile. It should be illegal for one person to be so gorgeous.

Orion's bladder screamed for him to get moving. With a barely suppressed sigh for the loss of Tucker's face, Orion slipped from bed as silently as possible. While in the bathroom, he went ahead and brushed his teeth. For a long minute he stared at his reflection in the mirror. Orion never made a point to look at himself. He never saw a collection of features, making up a person's face—like a normal person would. Orion saw his mother's eyes and his father's jaw. Dark hair from some anonymous source he would never know. There were very few times he recalled his parents being sober. Even less times when they were clean at the same time. The one thing Orion clearly recalled was finding them dead. Their empty, lifeless eyes staring at nothing. To his shame, he also recalled his relief. That is, until he realized no one else wanted him either. He would still go hungry, just under a different roof. Orion switched off the light. No good ever came from looking at himself.

Tucker still slept peacefully when Orion left the bathroom. He didn't have the heart to wake him. Instead, Orion grabbed a bottle of water from the kitchen and headed for his chair. He had a book waiting and time to kill. Hopefully, Tucker got the rest he obviously needed. That was all Orion had to offer. Thank goodness he had taken a vacation day. Otherwise, he might have ended up fired.

TUCKER PADDED TO THE BATHROOM, FINDING the toothbrush Orion kept for him there. He went through his usual morning routine, trying to shake off the death sleep he had endured. Somehow, it was three in the afternoon. The hours had passed in the blink of an eye. He wondered what time Orion had rolled from bed and why he hadn't woken him. Now, he only had a few hours left until he had another job tonight.

He found Orion in the same spot he had last night, except this time he stared at an open book. Orion had his bottom lip held between his teeth and eyes scanned the pages. He was so fucking perfect.

"There's the sexy man of my dreams. Why didn't you wake me up when you got up?"

Orion looked up from his book. Even though he focused on Tucker, Tucker could tell he was still half inside the book in his hands by his dazed expression. Tucker bit the inside of his cheek to hide his smile.

Orion blinked. "Hey. Did you have a good night of sleep?"

He was adorable. "Too good. I barely have any time left to spend with you now before I have to get ready to go out for work."

"Oh." Orion set his book aside. "I didn't realize you had a job tonight. I'll fix you something to drink. You're probably thirsty after sleeping forever."

Tucker shook his head as Orion headed for the kitchen. Even though Tucker was a dreamer, he still had never met anyone with their head in the clouds as much as Orion. Tucker couldn't get enough of him. Between his snark and his innocence, Orion was a treasure.

When Orion didn't return after several minutes, Tucker went hunting. He found Orion standing in the middle of the kitchen, staring at nothing, while the sink overflowed onto the floor.

Tucker rushed to turn off the water. "What are you doing? I thought you were fixing me something to drink."

Orion blinked. The way he looked at Tucker made Tucker wonder if his head was still half in another world. "Oh. Sorry." He blinked some more. "I was just thinking about this scene I read right before you woke up." He moved to the sink and opened the cabinet below it. He pulled out a few hand towels. Orion draped them over the puddle on the floor, letting them soak up the mess. "I think that scene was bullshit. It's bugging me."

Tucker's cheeks ached from smiling. Orion wasn't meant for this world. "Tell me about it. Maybe we can work it out."

While using his foot to mop up the mess with the towels, Orion spoke over his shoulder. "This girl was on the bed with her head hanging over the edge when the guy came in the room. He bent over and kissed her upside down. They were both super into it, but I can't think that would be anything but awkward. Like teeth licking and nose all in the chin awkward. I don't know. It's just bugging me."

"Okay. Well... let's go try it."

Orion snorted.

Tucker didn't back down. "I'm serious. You're my best friend. If you need to figure this out, it's my job to help you out. Let's try it."

Orion looked his way. He seemed two steps beyond shocked. "You think of me as your best friend?"

That wasn't what he expected had surprised Orion. The guy always kept Tucker on his toes. "Duh," Tucker said, rolling his eyes. "I spend all my free time with you. Why else would I do that?" He motioned Orion toward the bedroom. "Come on. Let's figure out the reality of this scene."

Orion didn't move. "But I don't know where your lips have been."

Sometimes, Orion really tested him. "Nowhere for at least a year now."

The skeptical expression Orion wore spoke volumes. "But you go on dates almost daily."

"No. I work. It's not the same. I'm not trying to really date anyone who hires me. Plus, it's only temporary. Pretty soon, Toby and I will back away and leave the guys we've been hiring to go on the actual dates. You know I don't need the money."

"Then why do you do it? I've always been curious."

Tucker waved off his question. "So the guys know we don't think we're too good to do what they do, and they feel comfortable enough to come to us if anything goes wrong. Toby and I will intercede by barring certain customers, filing restraining orders, or taking legal action. And don't think I don't see right through you, buddy. Stop changing the subject. Let's go see if that book is wrong so you can send them a strongly worded email or whatever it is you do when you find ridiculousness in books."

Orion's forehead furrowed. "I don't do that." He moved past Tucker, heading toward the bedroom. "I just won't read anything else by the author."

Tucker followed on Orion's heels, scared to hope. He wouldn't believe Orion truly meant to let Tucker kiss him until it happened.

Orion climbed onto the bed, flipped onto his back, and hung his head over the edge. He looked exactly like this was a science experiment. If there was an ounce of sexual desire in Orion for Tucker, he should win an award for his ability to hide it. This kiss would mean nothing to him while it meant everything to Tucker. Orion crossed his arms over his chest—like a martyr. "Okay. Let's do this."

Heat soared through Tucker's veins as he crossed the room. Each step he took in Orion's direction, Tucker's heart beat a little faster. He gently grasped Orion's throat as he bent. Tucker needed Orion to give him more than a half second kiss. He needed a moment to make Orion feel what he did. Tucker opened his mouth over Orion's bottom lip. Orion gasped. Tucker took advantage and licked Orion's tongue. His cock stirred, hardening as Orion licked him back. Tucker didn't hold back. He licked, sucked, and nibbled, pouring his heart into the only kiss he would probably ever get from Orion. Their kiss turned even more heated by the second. Tucker was so turned on that his entire body throbbed. He had to know if Orion was as aroused as him. Tucker massaged Orion's chest as he kissed him deep. He didn't give Orion time to guess at his intentions. Tucker copped a feel of Orion's cock, finding him hard. Tucker rubbed, fully intent on driving him insane. He needed Orion every bit as crazed as him.

Orion pulled his hair and bit him before ripping his face away. He openly gasped for air with his eyes squeezed shut. Tucker couldn't look away. Orion's chest expanded. His eyes opened, but he didn't look Tucker's way. "I guess that author knew what she was talking about, after all."

"Orion." Even Tucker heard the desperation in his voice.

Orion rolled from the bed, leaving Tucker behind on his knees.

With a deep breath for strength, Tucker pushed to his feet and went after Orion. He found him standing at the kitchen counter, staring at nothing again.

"Orion."

Orion barely glanced over his shoulder. "Are you hungry? I have hamburgers I could throw on the grill."

From nowhere, the backs of Tucker's eyes burned. Orion would never truly want him. All the months he had spent trying to win the guy were for nothing. Whatever reasons Orion had for ignoring what grew larger between them every day, Tucker couldn't breach them. He swallowed past the hurt. Tucker was pretty used to being unloved. It seemed his brothers were all he would ever have. "That's fine. I'll go get the grill started." He turned away, heading for the back door. No amount of talking would change anything. He would stick to why he had come here—being Orion's friend—and then he would go home. Maybe, he wouldn't come back though. His heart couldn't take the beating. Tucker had already spent most of his life getting his ass kicked. He had sworn, when his dad died, he wouldn't let anyone else hurt him. Being with Orion was starting to hurt. He couldn't keep doing it.

"Tucker."

Tucker turned at the sound of his name. For a moment, Orion looked as lost as Tucker felt. His shoulders fell and he looked away, as if looking at Tucker physically hurt him too. "You're my best friend too."

Well, fuck. Now, he didn't know what to do.

ORION HAD NO CLUE HOW MUCH TIME PASSED while he clung to the counter and stared at nothing. His body burned. Orion's heart was a mess. He had always known, if he ever let Tucker touch him, he wouldn't survive it. Orion couldn't explain what happened. One second, he had been ranting about that stupid book. The next, he had climbed onto the bed, completely prepared to get his heart wrecked. It was so much better than he had ever fantasized it would be. The pain was so much worse than he ever dreamed. There was no scenario where someone like Tucker fell for someone like him. Orion was a book nerd. He was skinny, awkward, and didn't know how to flirt. Orion was that guy who hid in the corner, incapable of making friends or small talk. Tucker was that cool kid. The one that got invited to every party. He had money and countless friends. Tucker could play sports in the morning and wear a tux to a huge event at night. His body, smile, and eyes were beautiful. Fuck, even his hands were sexy. Now, Orion knew his kiss was amazing too.

The way Tucker had kissed him and rubbed his body, Orion could still barely breathe. If Orion hadn't stopped, Tucker wouldn't have either. He could have been inside the man tonight. Orion drew a deep breath in through his nose. What then? He never would have seen Tucker again and that would kill Orion. Tucker was all he had. He realized Tucker didn't know it, but Orion's life was completely empty. He was an orphan who had survived a group home by losing himself in books. Dreaming was all he had. Only when the world disappeared into fiction, did Orion know what it was like to feel love. When he lived a thousand lives through stories, Orion wasn't alone. Tucker was the only real connection Orion had. If Tucker took away his friendship, maybe Orion would completely disappear.

Orion grabbed the hamburger patties and threw some spices on them, determined to push that kiss from his mind. Tucker reappeared. His hand slid across the small of Orion's back. The scent of his cologne overcame him. Orion's eyes fell closed as he sucked the smell into his lungs.

"I keep forgetting to tell you, I won't be around this weekend. There's a weekend long event I can't avoid."

Orion nodded. They were back on familiar ground. He could handle this part. Orion was used to Tucker spending time with other men. "That's fine. I don't expect you to always come around." He shrugged and kept his eyes locked on the food. "You have this whole life outside of me."

"No. Really, I don't."

Tucker sounded sad. Orion's gaze slid Tucker's way despite his best efforts. Tucker stared back at him, as if waiting for Orion's full attention. Alarm bells clanged in the back of Orion's mind. His brain screamed for him to run. Orion's feet refused to budge. Before Orion could react, Tucker was there. Tucker's body collided with his. Orion was trapped between the counter and Tucker's massive body. Every molecule of his body was on fire as Tucker's mouth came down hard on his. Orion automatically opened for him, practically begging. Tucker ate at his mouth while Orion couldn't do anything but match his intensity. His feet left the floor as Tucker lifted him by his ass, hauled him forward, and ground his erection against Orion's. For a moment, Orion's brain short-circuited. He was nothing more than wanton desire. Orion clung to Tucker's huge chest on the verge of shaking with need. Then, he felt something shift in his chest. Fear set in. His palms flattened against Tucker's chest. He pushed. Tucker's entire body hardened. It was as if he physically felt Tucker's heart close to him. His feet slipped back to the floor as Tucker set him away.

"Tucker." Even Orion heard the pleading in his voice. "We're just too different." Orion didn't understand how his tongue still worked. Yet there was no denying the idiocy falling from his lips. "You'll meet someone who matches you and I'll be left in the dust. This isn't one of my books where the nerd lands the hottest guy in town. It's real life." He couldn't stop. Words kept flowing out, making Orion want to bite off his tongue. "The first time someone questions why you're dating me, you'll be humiliated. Please, just let me be your friend. Stop trying for more. I don't want to get hurt. I just want your friendship." Orion's chin dropped. His gaze hit the floor. Orion's eyes burned with shame. "I just want to be your friend. That's as close as someone like me gets to really having someone like you."

"Wow." Tucker's voice sounded dead. It had Orion's chin shooting upward. He had to see Tucker's face. His expression didn't match. Tucker's eyes burned with rage. Orion was transfixed. "I had no idea. You honest to god think I'm a piece of shit, don't you?" He shook his head. A scary looking smile touched his lips. Orion would have taken a step back if he could. A humorless laugh rumbled from

Tucker. He shook his head again. Finally, he let out a long and exaggerated sigh. When his gaze locked on Orion again, Orion's skin went cold. Tucker was beyond enraged. "I spend all day working my ass off, so I'll be free when you get home. When I get hired for jobs, I watch the clock the whole time, waiting for the minute I can rush here to be with you. If I actually convince you to go somewhere with me, I try hard to stand as close as I can, because I'm so fucking proud for people to think you might be mine. And this whole goddamn time, you've been thinking you need to keep me in my place because I'm an egotistical ass who will fuck anything." Orion wanted to argue. His throat wouldn't work, and Tucker didn't give him a chance. Tucker took a step closer. His hips collided with Orion's body. Tucker's erection couldn't be missed. "Even knowing you think I'm the biggest piece of shit on the planet, I still want you. How stupid am I?"

His expression turned cruel and Orion's heart squeezed. He wanted to run as Tucker dipped his chin and got in his face, refusing to let Orion look away. "At least I know I'm fucked up, Orion. I know that over a decade of living in a tent while my dad kicked me, spit on me, and knocked out my teeth fucked me up in the head. I'm well aware that I'm worthless, but I never, ever expected that you—someone just as broken but completely blind to it—would be the one to break me even more." He stroked Orion's jaw. "You are incredibly beautiful and equally blind, but I'm just some asshole who doesn't care, right?" He pushed away, as if he ripped away his friendship along with his body. Orion felt it break. "I won't waste anymore of your time. I'm sorry I hung around where I wasn't wanted." He walked away, leaving Orion empty, and with no clue how to fix it. Tucker was right. Orion was broken. No one had ever taught him how to love. Now, losing everything, Orion was a master at that. Some things never changed.

FOUR

TO ORION'S AMAZEMENT, he made it until right before lunchtime before he couldn't take another second of not talking to Tucker. He missed Tucker's ridiculous plans to make him leave the house, and his big goofy smile. Orion was dying inside without Tucker's stupid texts with even dumber jokes. He felt the void where Tucker should be every second of the day.

Orion dug his cellphone out of his desk. He didn't know what to say, so he stuck with something simple.

Orion: *I figure you're probably just now waking up, so good morning. I'm sorry about everything.*

For several minutes, he stared at his phone, mentally willing it to buzz with an incoming text.

Nothing happened. His eyes burned from not blinking. At least, that's what he told himself. He tore his gaze away and went back to work while trying desperately to focus on anything other than the silent phone sitting on his desk. His chest felt heavy—like the air in his office was too thick. He sniffed. Orion bit his bottom lip, fighting the wave of misery that threatened to engulf him. He thought his mind might snap.

"David wants an update on that Winston and Church street project." Kyle let himself into Orion's office like he owned the place. He plopped down in the chair across from Orion's desk. "Why do you keep your office door closed? No one else does that."

Orion didn't look away from his computer screen. He wasn't sure he didn't look every bit as ready to cry as he was. "The Winston and Church project is on schedule. I'll have it done by next Wednesday, as promised. My office door is closed because Simon listens to shit music while Rachel gossips about everything under the sun and I can hear all of it very clearly. If that wasn't enough, Hugh has porn playing on his computer screen a majority of the day which reflects right into my office when the door is open, and I also just like being left alone."

Kyle chuckled, as if he either hadn't heard a word Orion said or thought he was joking. "You should come out with us tonight. We're going to the Roadhouse for steak and bottomless beer."

A hint of guilt sneaked in at Kyle's offer. His co-workers were always inviting him out, but Orion never went, except for the one time he ditched them at Howling Twister, but whatever. At least this time he had a good excuse. "I'm sorry. I have other plans."

For a long moment, Kyle stared at him in silence. His dark blue gaze moved over Orion's face, looking for something Orion couldn't decipher. He slid lower in his seat and steepled his fingers, looking a tiny bit wicked. Kyle was a good-looking guy. Orion wasn't immune, but they worked together. "If you're uncomfortable with crowds, you should let me take you someplace quiet for dinner instead."

Kyle's offer stunned Orion for a second. He had always admired Kyle's perfectly styled sandy blond hair and put together appearance, but still. "I wasn't blowing you off when I said I already have plans. I'm leaving right after work for San Antonio."

"Oh." Kyle straightened in his chair. "What's in San Antonio?"

"A book convention. Some of my favorite authors will be there. I have a weekend pass." To Orion's surprise, Kyle didn't turn condescending like most men tended to do when he showed his nerdy side.

"That truly sounds like your kind of thing. I hope you have a good time. How about a rain check? Maybe when you get back?"

Orion nodded. "I don't see why not." After all, it wasn't like Orion had anything else since Tucker was done with him now. Plus, even though Kyle was handsome, Orion didn't feel completely out of his league with the guy. Kyle smiled, looking triumphant. Orion's heart sank. He didn't feel out of his league because he felt nothing at all. Orion returned Kyle's smile to hide the emptiness growing inside. Tucker was right. He was a fucked-up mess, and he was too scared to admit it.

FOR TEN MINUTES, TUCKER LISTENED TO HIS phone's occasional buzz in the cup holder. Finally, while stopped at a red light, he broke. As he read Orion's casual "I'm sorry," he ground his back teeth to a pulp. The thing was, he was mad at himself. Orion had never tried to be more than friends with Tucker. Hell, for a while there, he didn't even try to be friends with Tucker. It was Tucker who kept trying for more. Yet, he had gotten in Orion's face, and accused him of being too fucked up to try. Tucker was so angry with himself he didn't know where to start. He thought—maybe—he should start by going away.

Tucker knew he was the problem. Orion deserved to be free of him. He wanted Orion to be happy. If he really loved Orion, it was time to get out of his way. His heart broke a little more as the seconds ticked by while he ignored Orion's text. His only excuse was that he had never been in love. Maybe he didn't know how to do it right.

The moment he parked, he snatched up his phone. He would leave Orion in peace, but he wouldn't leave him alone if he needed someone.

Tucker: *If Orion stops by while I'm out of town, will you keep him company if you're home? He might be upset.*

Toby: *Yeah, if I'm here. What did you do?*

That was the thing, wasn't it? He was such a fuck up, even his brothers knew it was his fault.

Tucker: *Too much to type in a text. I'll tell you about it later. Maybe you can tell me what I should do.*

Toby: *I'm the oldest. That's my job.*

With a shake of his head, Tucker snorted and

threw open his truck door. Toby prided himself on being the oldest. The thing was, he was also the most well-adjusted. That had nothing to do with the nine-minute head start on life he had over Tucker. Toby was the one who never stayed quiet. He was the one who spoke up. The one who tried to keep them safe as kids by drawing attention his way. He was the one who had made the tough choices and saved them in the end. Maybe Tucker still needed a bit more saving. Tucker never stopped feeling like he was drowning.

FIVE

THE HOTEL IN SAN ANTONIO, where the convention was being held, was bustling with people. The place was old and grand looking, selling itself as one of the most haunted hotels in the country. Orion didn't care about any of that. Not only did he not believe in ghosts, he just needed a place to sleep and shower.

After checking in and dropping his luggage at his room, Orion grabbed his ticket to the event and headed downstairs. He tried waiting on the elevator, but after ten minutes passed, he gave up and hit the stairs. By following the signs through several hallways, Orion easily found the room to sign in. He traded his ticket for a lanyard with his name tag and a welcome bag full of god knows what. He didn't want to stand there and dig to find out.

Orion barely got the lanyard draped around his neck before a tall guy with thick blond hair and glasses stepped into his path. He eyed Orion's name tag. "Orion. Love the name. Where are you from?"

"Here," Orion said, trying not to get distracted by the combination of dark blue eyes and hint of hairy chest peeking out at him. "Well, not here, here. I live in Austin, so just down the road."

"Me too. Well, not Austin, but not far from there. New Braunfels."

Orion nodded. "That's a pretty town. Are you here to see a particular author or just for the love of books?"

His new friend lifted the badge hanging around his neck and twirled it, so the name tag faced forward. "Actually, I'm an author. Mister Haven."

Orion smiled. "Is that your real name? Mister sounds suspiciously made up."

He winked. "So does Orion."

"Touché. Nice to meet you, Mister."

Mister's dimples deepened. His expression turned wicked. "I'll admit that sounds damn sexy on your lips." Before Orion had time to puzzle over his words or discomfort could set in, Mister motioned toward the open doorway behind him. "Everyone is playing book boyfriend bingo right now. Would you like to sit together?"

"Sounds good," Orion said with a sharp nod. As he followed Mister to a nearby table, Orion mused over how comfortable he felt. Everyone smiled as he sat down at the already crowded table. They pushed some bingo cards and candy his way. Normally, he felt out of place everywhere he went, but these people were just like him. They were here because they loved to read. Orion could breathe for the first time in a long time. Tucker wasn't the only thought in his head, and it was freeing.

Mister leaned his way. "So, did you come this weekend to meet anyone in particular or are you looking for new authors?"

"Both," Orion admitted. "I'm always on the lookout for new authors, but I also saw that T.J. Brown would be here, selling advanced copies of his book that's set to release next month. He's one of my favorites, so I hoped to snag one before they sell out."

While arranging his cards, Mister nodded. "T.J. is here already. I saw him earlier. You might be able to convince him to sell you a copy before the signing tomorrow. Technically, that's against signing policy, but meh. You paid to be here, so you can ask, right?"

He glanced around the room before focusing on Orion. "He said something about coming down for the games tonight, but I'm not sure he will. The bigger names don't always hang out at all the events. They worry readers won't give the rest of us a chance if they attend everything."

That made sense. Orion had to admit, if he knew T.J. was there right now, he might try to steal a moment of his time. "What do you write?"

Dark blue eyes filled with good humor flashed his way at Orion's question. "BDSM how-to books." Orion's eyebrows rose. Mister kept talking. "I'm giving a live demo later tonight." He winked. "If you're interested."

Orion caught himself smiling. "Maybe I'll see you there."

"Oh, there's T.J.," a woman muttered nearby, snagging Orion's attention.

Orion turned his head. Tucker filled the doorway. His sexy forest green eyes scanned the room. He looked unhappy. His gaze landed on Orion. For a moment, they held each other's stare. Tucker turned and walked away.

"I guess he decided not to stay," the woman added, as Tucker disappeared.

Orion's frozen brain clicked the two statements

together. Tucker was T.J. What the hell? Orion flew to his feet, snatching up his welcome bag as he went. "Excuse me." He didn't even know who he was talking to exactly. All Orion knew was, he was pissed as hell, and he needed to catch Tucker. In the hallway, he spotted Tucker's retreating form. His short legs had a hell of a time trying to keep up with Tucker's long stride. Orion would be goddamned if he ran through the halls like a crazy person. His temper broke.

"Tucker Jonas Kodiak. Are you running from me?"

Tucker froze in his tracks. He turned, wearing a scowl. "Did you just call me to the carpet, using my full name?"

Orion didn't back down. "Maybe I did, T.J. Brown. That's clever, by the way, being as how a Kodiak is just a brown bear." Pain sliced through Orion's chest. "I guess I know how you managed to get me that personalized copy of *Redemption Highway* for my last birthday." Orion's voice cracked. His gaze skirted away as he closed the distance between them. "Do I even know you at all?"

The hard edge to Tucker's voice didn't soften when he answered. "I don't know. Did you ever try to know me? Or were you too busy trying to keep me in my place to be bothered?"

Defeat washed over Orion. Not only had he obviously never known Tucker, Tucker was openly done with Orion. The small peace he had found by coming here was gone. Orion shook his head. He fought the darkness he had avoided since meeting Tucker. It was so fucking hard to breathe. "Never mind. Forget you saw me here." He stepped around Tucker and headed for the elevator. As he pushed the button, calling for the lift, he felt Tucker move to stand beside him. They stood side by side in silence. Neither of them made any move to talk. They felt even more finished than before. Maybe he would just go home. There would be no peace here now.

Orion stared hard at the frozen lit number above the elevator door. He willed it to move and set him free from this hell, while barely suppressing the urge to tap his foot. Nervousness took control of his tongue. "I had this problem earlier. With it being this close to dinnertime, everyone is probably trying to get on the elevator at the same time to come downstairs. Maybe I should just take stairs."

"I never take the stairs," Tucker said, sounding absent.

Orion's forehead furrowed in confusion. He felt

it happen. Tucker had stairs in his house and his bedroom was literally at the top of his staircase. His words didn't make sense. "Why?"

Tucker flashed him an unreadable look. "Because they're always *up* to something."

Out of the blue, Orion's throat swelled, and his eyes burned. "You can't stop being my friend. You're all I have," Orion said, hearing the way his voice gave away his barely suppressed tears. Orion tore his gaze away and went back to staring at the closed doors. The burning behind his eyes intensified. The doors blurred. Orion broke and turned away, heading for the stairs. He couldn't do this. Everything hurt too badly. He didn't know why he had chased after Tucker. They weren't friends anymore. Tucker could keep his secrets, since Orion obviously didn't matter that much. Orion barely cleared the door to the stairwell when Tucker overcame him. His large body collided with Orion's back, knocking the air from his lungs.

Tucker snatched him off his feet and held Orion so tightly against his chest that Orion couldn't catch his breath. Of course, he recognized it might be his broken heart and not Tucker's hold, choking him. Tucker's lips brushed the shell of his ear. Air filled Orion's lungs. He clung to the arms wrapped around him—like they were his only lifeline.

Tucker made a shushing noise against his ear. "Shhh. It's okay. We're okay." He kissed Orion's ear again. "I don't understand you, baby," Tucker said, keeping his voice soothing. "Why are you so convinced that I can't be your friend and be in love with you? I've been pulling off both just fine for months now." He kissed Orion's neck. "Just come upstairs with me, okay? I promise everything will be okay. Let me fix it."

Orion went limp in Tucker's arms. He didn't have the strength to fight. Orion didn't have the power to control anything. All he knew was, he couldn't be without Tucker. He didn't have anything else.

Tucker kept one eye on Orion while they climbed the stairs to the third floor. He looked so dejected and broken that Tucker half expected him to drop. He had done that. Tucker's throat tightened. While standing outside the elevator, Orion looked exactly like a man drowning on dry land. He had never hurt worse, and that was saying a lot. Hurting Orion, it was a hot poker in his heart.

"I'm in 316."

Orion nodded as they cleared the doorway to the third floor. Still, he kept his head down as he walked. Tucker dug his keycard from his wallet. He had no idea what to do or say. All he knew was, he couldn't lose Orion or keep hurting him. This was horrible.

As they reached the door, Orion sniffed. Tucker froze at the sound. He snagged Orion's chin, forcing his face Tucker's way. His eyes were red and filled with tears. Tucker swore he heard his heart crack. He pressed his lips to Orion's, because he had to. Orion didn't flinch or pull away. He let it happen.

Tucker scanned his card and herded Orion into the room. The moment the door closed behind them, Tucker snatched Orion off his feet and claimed his mouth. Orion tossed his welcome bag to the floor and came back at him every bit as hard. He pulled Tucker's hair as he tried climbing his body. Tucker lifted him higher with both hands full of Orion's ass. Orion wrapped his legs around Tucker's waist and held on. Even though Tucker was more turned on than he had ever been in his life, his heart was the organ in charge.

He took Orion down on the bed. Orion tore at

Tucker's clothes. Tucker leaned away to let Orion have his shirt. Orion lifted, following him. The moment Tucker's chest was bared, Orion's teeth sank into his pec. Tucker could barely breathe. Lust choked him. He should have known Orion would be like a wildcat, tearing at his skin. Tucker threw his head back and sucked air as Orion ripped open the front of Tucker's jeans and dove in. He massaged Tucker's cock like he had every intention of getting covered in cum that minute.

"Holy shit. Slow down. You feel way too good."

"That's the point," Orion growled while nibbling every spot he could reach. "I don't have anything with me, so this is the best I can do until later."

"There's lube and condoms in your welcome bag."

Orion went still. "Are you serious?"

Tucker nodded as he went to work on removing Orion's clothes. "They're stamped with my name."

"Thank god," Orion breathed, pushing Tucker's jeans down his hips. In a tumble of stolen kisses and ripping of clothes, they finally managed to get undressed. Sweat already coated Tucker's skin from the effort it took not to snap like a wild animal. He knew from their many candid late-night talks that they were both pretty versatile, but Tucker had teased many times he would gladly let Orion fuck him. Tucker wanted that now. He was pretty much dying for the dick at this point, especially now that he knew how rough Orion would be. There were already several scratches and bite marks marring his skin. Tucker needed more. Later, they could go slow.

He dove for the box of condoms and lube he had brought with him to hand out as promotional items. Tucker was thankful he had them. If he missed this, it would kill him. He handed the condom to Orion while he ripped open the packet of lube. Clear liquid went everywhere in his impatience. Orion's mouth came down on his before Tucker could do anything else. His bottom lip stung as Orion's teeth sank into it. A moan vibrated through him. His thoughts scattered.

"I want you on your stomach. You have no idea how much I love your sexy back. I want to bite it while I fuck you."

Jesus. Tucker couldn't catch his breath. He had always known Orion was sexy and straightforward, but he had been unprepared for this dominant confidence. Tucker immediately rolled. He would do anything.

"Goddamn. Look at you," Orion said, running his hands down Tucker's back until he could squeeze his ass. His thumbs traced Tucker's crack, massaging, and teasing. "You're even sexier than I ever imagined, and I've done a lot of fantasizing. Do you? Have you jacked off with my name on your lips?"

Tucker moaned. He couldn't hold back the sound. "Yes. Always."

Orion's hands disappeared. Tucker whimpered and they were back. Wet fingers found his asshole. Tucker humped the bed like a wanton. Orion teased. He fingered the spot between Tucker's balls and hole and circled his asshole with no penetration. Tucker bit the sheets in his frustration.

"You have no idea how beautiful you are to me," Orion said, nearly whispering. "I know you're gorgeous and that you know it, but to me, you're absolutely perfect. Flawless." His fingertip slipped inside Tucker. "You're like a book. A fantasy." He urged Tucker's knees apart. "Except you're real, and you're mine right now." Orion's crown brushed his asshole. Tucker fought the urge to beg. Then, Orion began pushing inside. Tucker scratched at the sheets. He was wide, stretching Tucker to the point he almost backed down. Without warning, Orion thrust. His hips slammed against Tucker's ass. Tucker saw stars. Orion rocked at the perfect angle, hitting the internal button that had pre-cum soaking the mattress beneath him.

"Oh my god. Oh, fuck."

Orion rocked again, slowly massaging the perfect spot.

Tucker writhed, fucking the bed, and uncaring if he looked every bit as desperate as he felt. "Please?" The harsh whisper sounded like Tucker was on the verge of tears. He thought he might be. Tucker had never wanted anything more in his life than he wanted Orion's dick.

Orion growled. Tucker's stomach muscles clenched at the sound. That was all the warning he got before Orion fucked him. There was no other description for the bruising thrusts that had his ass leaving the bed or the solid pounding against his prostate. Tucker held the sheets in an iron grip while cries ripped from his throat. Orion's short nails and teeth tore at his skin while he completely destroyed Tucker's asshole. Tucker fucked the mattress like a horny teenage boy, uncaring of what he screwed as long as he got that orgasm. Ecstasy owned him—like its bitch. He pleaded and cried, begging for more and swearing his life to Orion. Tucker would be on his knees every night, worshipping Orion. He would fall on this altar forever for more of this.

"Goddamn." Pressure built to the point of madness. Tucker openly rocked against the mattress, needing release.

Orion hit a steady pace right where Tucker needed him. "Come. Now," Orion demanded.

Tucker focused everything on his needs. An explosion of pure bliss moved Tucker's soul. Every thought floated away as he stayed suspended in a moment of unadulterated pleasure. Waves of ecstasy poured from his cock. His entire body jerked uncontrollably.

A loud cry sounded against his skin as Orion took his pleasure from Tucker. In that moment, Tucker was complete in a way he had never experienced. Orion had rocked him to his core.

The moment Orion collapsed beside him in a panting mess, Tucker struck. Air meant nothing. He needed Orion's kiss to survive. The moment their tongues met, Orion buried his fingers in Tucker's hair, and Tucker softened.

"I love you," Tucker whispered between kisses. Even to his ears he sounded winded and moved. "Not just as a friend. I'm in love with you. Always have been."

Orion nodded and massaged his scalp. "I love

you too. I'm sorry we fought. You mean everything to me. I don't ever want to lose you."

"You can't," Tucker swore, going back for more kisses. Orion was an addiction that kept Tucker high and coming back. He was a sticky mess and the bed was soaked. As much as he didn't care, he needed Orion to be comfortable so maybe he would stay. "Let's fix the bed. I want to hold you for a little while."

With a nod, Orion rolled from the bed. He headed for the bathroom to get rid of the condom. While he was gone, Tucker did the best he could with the bed, covering the wet sheet with a blanket before finding another blanket in the closet. Orion came back with a wet washcloth. Tucker held still while Orion cleaned his skin. He was still semi hard and working on another erection with Orion touching him.

Orion tossed the washcloth aside and met his stare. He looked as blown away as Tucker felt. "I missed you this morning." He visibly swallowed. "I didn't realize how bad it would hurt, having you ignore my texts."

Tucker swept Orion off his feet and into the bed. He crawled in beside him and settled down before pulling Orion into his arms. "I'm an idiot. It was like ripping my heart out when I didn't respond. I think we've established we're pretty necessary to each other. Let's not do that again."

With a nod, they fell silent. For a long while, they quietly enjoyed each other, stealing kisses and touches. They reveled in their new dynamic. This was the real version of them—together as one. Their love had always been there, waiting.

Orion flattened his palm against Tucker's, as if measuring the difference in size. "You know what's odd to me? I don't understand why you kept the T.J. Brown thing a secret. That's literally the reason we met. The night Tanner came to my house, he picked up one of your books, and said, 'I've read this one. It's good.' He didn't say his brother wrote it, which might have worked as an awesome pickup line with someone like me. He just said he'd read it. But still, that's the only reason I showed up the next day. He had chosen one of my favorite books, out of all the books in my den, to say he liked. After four months of knowing each other, and you giving me a personalized copy of one of your books for my birthday, you still never said a word. It's like you're ashamed. And when do you even have time to write? You're always with me or doing something with Cubs for Rent."

Tucker stared at the ceiling while toying with Orion's fingers. He trusted Orion. With everything. "I write during the day while you're at work," he said, tackling the last part first. That was the least complicated part. The rest started and ended where everything did—with his childhood in hell. "I always wanted to be a writer. Even before I was old enough to write, I would draw pictures, staple them together, sit in my mom's lap, and tell her the story that went along with each page." He smiled at the memory. Tucker had so few good ones. "When people ask me what I do, there's a part of me that wants to brag. My books have done amazing. I never thought anyone would buy them. But those books are also my soul exposed for the world. They were cathartic." Tucker swallowed hard. He was in love with Orion. The guy should know what he was getting. "And my Decade in Hell series is almost completely true. I just changed enough details that no one would know they were my brothers and my story. But I think, if people knew I'd written them, they might wonder if they're true. I don't want that."

Orion was so still, Tucker wondered if he had stopped breathing. After a moment, he took a ragged sounding breath. "But the dad in that story..."

"Yeah." Even Tucker heard the discomfort in his

voice. He never talked about that part of his life. The years when his dad had gone crazy, taken his children into the woods for over ten years, and hidden them from the world. His dad had been a famous baseball player. When he had retired, he had hit the drugs hard and his kids even harder. He had cheated on his wife with everything and anything moving until Tucker's mom had died to get away from him. Then, the real hell had started.

"I found my parents dead of a drug overdose when I was twelve," Orion said, surprising Tucker. He had never asked about Orion's family. Not because he didn't care, but because Tucker didn't even think about it. Sometimes, he simply forgot other people might have normal people they saw on the holidays. Orion had never mentioned a family, so Tucker hadn't asked. Plus, he didn't want to talk about his. So, it was a topic best avoided on all fronts. He didn't press now either. Tucker waited. Orion took another strained sounding breath. "They never hurt me. It was more like I wasn't there. I guess I wasn't, to them. They were in whatever world their high created. Meanwhile, I was in the background lonely, starving, and barely hanging on. My only saving grace was that we lived in this tiny-ass hotel room right down the road from the library. Every day

I would go there and read until they threw me out at closing time. I found them dead on a Sunday. The only day the library was closed." Orion paused, as if lost in thought, before sighing. "I suppose I should be grateful they died and no one else wanted me. Being an orphan in a group home who made straight A's landed me enough scholarships to get my engineering degree. So, there's that."

Tucker brought Orion's hand to his mouth and kissed his fingertips. "You know, when we first met, I would've sworn you were no more than eighteen. You looked so young and fragile until I looked into your eyes."

Orion chuckled. "Then you saw all the rage of a twenty-seven-year-old man."

"No," Tucker said, tracing his lips with Orion's fingers. "I saw fire and hoped you were a grown man because I knew I had to have you." He turned his head and met Orion's stare. "I knew I wouldn't stop until you were mine. You know I'm not the least bit sane, right? I'm extremely needy."

Orion didn't as much as blink. "Good."

"You'll never have any peace again."

One side of Orion's lips lifted in a half smile. It was sexy as fuck. "I'm looking forward to it."

"I'm also a jealous mess."

Orion pushed up onto his elbow and leaned Tucker's way. "That's sexy." He kissed Tucker before he could say more. Tucker knew Orion might think it was sexy now, but he had never seen Tucker come unglued. Everything he had said was the truth. When Tucker melted down, it was ugly as hell. He hoped Orion truly understood. They were together now. He would destroy anything or anyone who tried to come between them, even if it was himself.

SIX

WATCHING Tucker sign books while people fawned over him was hot as hell. Still, anytime Tucker had a moment when he wasn't talking or smiling, his jaw wouldn't stop flexing like he ground his teeth. The second they were alone, Orion broke.

"The muscle in your cheek is jumping. The way it always does when you're impatient to be done with something."

Tucker flashed him a smile. "I'm ready to be alone with you."

Orion bit his lip and dropped his gaze to the floor. He knew his smile was out of control. A sexy chuckle rumbling from Tucker had his chin lifting once more.

"Your embarrassment is sexy. Before today, I don't think I've ever seen you blush."

Heat exploded through Orion's face, as if his body was set to prove Tucker right. "I feel like everyone is staring at me, wondering why I'm sitting here with you."

Even though the crowd had finally died down and no one was at Tucker's table, Tucker grabbed a copy of his book and started writing inside. "You're working as my assistant. If anyone is staring at you, it's because you're sexy." He closed the book and held it out to Orion. "I know that's why I keep catching Mister Haven watching you. For you," he added when Orion didn't immediately take the book. His eyes flashed with wicked intent. "I hope you enjoy Ryan and Trevor's love story. It was a lot of fun for me to write."

Orion took the book with raised eyebrows. "Did you write us a love story?"

Tucker's smile was evil to say the least. He shrugged. "I guess you'll have to read it to find out."

Orion shook his head and flipped open the book. The author note at the beginning stared up at him.

I don't believe in Heaven, because I can't see it, and no god has ever tried to save me. I believe in

Orion, though. Now, that's true beauty. A real hero. The next best thing to Heaven.

His throat swelled as his eyes dropped to what Tucker had written below the passage.

For Orion, the love of my life. The family I chose —T.J. Brown

Orion had to clear his throat before meeting Tucker's stare again. "This is awesome. I love you."

The way Tucker stared back at him with his heart in his eyes and pride in his smile, Orion was moved. He needed to find something to do besides staring at Tucker like a lovesick fool. "Can I get you something to drink? I have a couple of books I want to buy before everyone packs up."

"I'm good. Just kiss me before you go, so Mister knows his place before you buy his book."

Orion couldn't stop smiling. "Admit it. You know you want me to buy his kinkiest BDSM book."

"Oh, I absolutely do," Tucker said without missing a beat. "I just want you to kiss me first."

A snort of laughter escaped Orion as he stood. He brushed a quick kiss across Tucker's lips before Tucker could press for more. The way Tucker's eyes flashed with humor, let Orion know he was right to move fast. Orion held tightly to his book as he headed out. He didn't want to risk anyone getting his copy. Orion was ridiculously happy. He didn't know if it would last or if he could withstand the crushing blow if it didn't. But Orion knew he had to try to make a go of this, because he was in love with Tucker. He probably had always been.

Mister's smile grew as Orion approached his table. "I see you got to meet T.J."

Orion fought a blush. "Actually, it turns out I already knew him. That's why I was so shocked when he walked through the door yesterday. Sorry about running out on you and for missing your demo last night. I still fully intend to buy a book though." He eyed Mister's table. It seemed he had several books. Orion didn't know where to start. He wasn't really the BDSM sort, but he wasn't opposed to trying a few things. "Which do you recommend?"

At his question, Mister sat forward. A wicked smile stretched his lips. At that moment, Orion could absolutely see Mister bringing someone to their knees. He could picture Mister making someone crawl. "Take this one," Mister said, grabbing a book and scrawling a few words inside before handing it over.

Orion absently flipped it open. "How much do I owe you?"

"It's on me."

"Awww, thank you." He read what Mister wrote inside. *Orion, check out the chapter on orgasm denial. I think you would be great at making men beg— Mister Haven.* Orion smiled. "I imagine you're used to hearing men beg." No one was more surprised than Orion over his words. He wasn't one to say every thought in his head.

To his surprise, Mister's smile turned sad. "No. Not anymore. Nowadays, I only do demos at conventions and write books. I no longer play for personal pleasure."

"Why?" The question popped out without permission. Orion scrambled after it. "If you don't mind me asking, that is."

Mister sat back, visibly relaxing. It was obvious he was unbothered by Orion's nosiness. He brushed his bottom lip with his fingertips in an absent motion, seeming to turn inward. "I had the perfect sub once. Seriously, he was... flawless." Mister's eyes cleared. He focused on Orion. "I fucked up and lost him. Now, I only do this for money. No sex involved."

A thought hit Orion. He set his books aside and dug out his wallet, finding a card. He explained as he went. "There's a company in Austin—Cubs for Rent. They are quickly becoming the biggest provider of different escort services in this area." He handed

Mister the card. "If you're ever looking for extra work, you should give them a call. They might be interested in listing your services on their site. I could see a bunch of rich people hosting parties where you do the demos and they drink too much. It could be a lucrative deal for you. Rich people love throwing scandalous parties."

A playful glint entered Mister's eyes as he accepted the card. "Are you listed on their site?"

Orion rolled his eyes. "I'm friends with the owners. No one would pay to date me."

"I would pay to do a lot with you." His gaze slid past Orion before slipping back his way. "I don't think I'm the only one. May I give you a bit of unsolicited advice?" He didn't wait for Orion to agree. "You only get one great passion. People can fall in love with countless people throughout their lives, but you only get one all-consuming connection. Don't let yours slip away." He surreptitiously nodded Tucker's way. "He wants to rip out my spine, because you've stood here too long, and he knows I want you. Don't let that get away."

Orion had no intentions of letting go. When he had climbed Tucker like a tree yesterday, Orion was making a conscious choice. He would hold on to this thing with Tucker with both hands until Tucker ripped away his love. Orion fully intended to jump in with both feet and give this everything. He had to. Orion had already found out he couldn't live without Tucker. If he hoped to survive losing him, Orion had to know that he had done everything humanly possible to keep him. He had to know it wasn't his fault if Tucker left.

IN ALL THE TIME TUCKER HAD KNOWN ORION, he had never seen the man more relaxed. He smiled and chatted with Mister like they were old friends. Mister visibly ate up every second of Orion's undivided attention. Tucker wanted to believe he was the reason Orion looked so soft and happy. The possessive beast inside him wanted to rip off Mister's arms and beat him to death with them. He had his dad's temper. Sometimes, he had to remind himself of that.

With a final wave, Orion turned away from Mister and headed in Tucker's direction. He held up the book he had gotten on the sly and waggled his eyebrows. The growling and snapping of teeth inside his head became a satisfied purr as Orion closed the distance between them. No one else existed for Tucker. They may as well have been alone.

"The art of erotic massage and orgasm denial. Nice. Well, the massage part, anyhow," Tucker said as Orion reclaimed his earlier seat. "I could do without the orgasm denial."

Orion winked as he tucked his books inside a canvas bag. "I gave Mister a card for Cubs for Rent. Don't worry. I didn't mention you, but I was thinking, he would be great for like parties or whatever. I imagine people would pay a lot to spend time with a BDSM master. The scandal," Orion said wickedly.

That was a good idea. "My sexy genius." Orion beamed at the praise. Tucker wanted to give him everything. "There's not much to pack up and I'm sold out of books now. Should we start gathering our stuff? I have plans for you."

Orion stood and worked on pulling Tucker's cart out from where it was hidden beneath the cloth covered table. "Do I get to know these plans?"

While holding Orion's gaze, Tucker nodded. "First, I plan to fuck you. Then, I'll take you to a nice dinner. Afterward, we'll come back here, and I'll make love to you until you fall into an exhausted and useless heap."

"This sounds like a solid and well thought out plan."

Tucker chuckled at Orion's serious tone. He was so ridiculously in love with this sexy weirdo. He couldn't wait to have him alone. Tucker had never been more scared in his life that he would wake up and find out his happiness was all a dream. His life had been too hard. Orion was the one thing he could not lose.

Tucker tried not to grind his back teeth on the way to the elevator, since Orion had already called him on it once. He was just damn impatient to have Orion alone. Several people stopped them along the way, asking Tucker questions about upcoming books and his plans for the night. Tucker smiled, nodded, and answered as much as he could.

Standing outside the elevator doors, Tucker considered throwing a fit. They had already learned from several back-and-forth trips that waiting on the elevator was a lesson in patience. The hotel was large and only had two, and if everyone was trying to get somewhere at the same time—like authors and readers all leaving an event at the same time—it was better to take the stairs. Unfortunately, even though Tucker had sold out of books, he still had too much stuff on a cart to carry up three flights of stairs.

By the time the door slid open, ten people stepped out, and he got his cart loaded onto the elevator, Tucker was ready to scream. When the doors closed behind them, Tucker lost what little patience he had left. One look at the sexy eyes that had ensnared him at first sight, and Tucker snagged Orion by the back of the neck. He hauled Orion forward and captured his mouth. Tucker didn't hold back. He poured months of longing into their kiss. The pressure in his chest eased. With one final nibble of Orion's bottom lip, Tucker pulled away.

"I've been wanting to do that all day."

"I'm happy to be of service," Orion said, sounding serious and making Tucker laugh. Orion was completely unique. It was obvious he didn't truly know how much power he held over Tucker. He didn't get that Tucker had never loved anyone else. Orion didn't see that Tucker would go to any length to please him, but he would. Tucker had every intention of being so far beneath Orion's skin that Orion couldn't escape him. He had been waiting too long. No more. Tucker planned to steal Orion's world.

SEVEN

THE HOUR and a half drive from San Antonio to Austin turned into two hours thanks to the church-releasing-and-headed-to-lunch-afterward rush hour. It turned out, two hours was exactly two hours too long for Tucker to be alone with his thoughts. He wanted more. While Tucker was ninety-eight-point-eight percent completely batshit insane, and he recognized it had only been four months, he wanted everything with Orion. The past four months had been grueling, backbreaking, and soul crushingly filled with longing on his end.

Now that Orion had touched him, Tucker wanted to unleash all the crazy. He was already wondering how much longer he had to wait before he could start moving Orion's stuff to his place. He knew which room they could turn into a library. Christmas wasn't that far away. Would Orion feel cheated out of a real gift if Tucker used the occasion to propose? He could buy him more gifts than just that. Tucker smiled, uncaring if he looked crazy. He could take Orion to Aspen for Christmas. Tucker had never been, but he wanted to go. He liked snow. Sort of. In theory. It didn't snow in Austin very often, and when it did, it wasn't much.

His smile fell. All those plans were insane, right? Orion would rightfully run for the hills if Tucker sprang all that insanity on him. He made it until he was sitting in his garage. Tucker snatched up his cellphone and dialed Orion's number. He didn't bother with hellos when he answered.

"Hang up if you're still driving."

A gorgeous chuckle brushed his ear. "I'm home. I'm just now dragging everything in the house."

"Hey, speaking of your house, do you rent or own?"

"Um. I rent. Why?" Orion sounded adorably confused.

"When is your lease up?" He covered his eyes. "Never mind. Can I come over?"

"What's going on, baby? Don't you need to see

your brothers and find out your scheduled appointments and all that?"

Tucker bit back a growl. He didn't want to be an adult today. "Yeah. I guess." Tucker perked up again. "Grab some clothes and come stay here with me tonight. You know my brothers love you and I love you and I want you here." Yeah. He wasn't needy at all.

Orion was silent for so long Tucker expected to get shot down. "Give me a couple of hours, okay?" Orion finally said. "I have some laundry to do and whatnot, but I'll get there as fast as I can."

The tension drained from Tucker's shoulders. "Okay. I'll be waiting."

"I love you."

Tucker couldn't resist the happiness in Orion's voice. "I love you too. See you soon."

"See ya," Orion said, disconnecting their call.

"This is certainly a different tone than the one you left town with," Toby said, appearing out of nowhere.

Tucker fought a blush. "Yeah. I guess so. He was at the book conference."

Toby blinked before a huge grin spread across his face. "So, you finally told him about your alter ego, huh? I told you he would love that."

"Actually, he was furious to the point I didn't think we'd be okay there for a minute when he first found out. It looked like keeping secrets was going to be the thing that finally pushed him over the edge with me. It worked out, though." Tucker felt his smile grow. "It ended up being a damn good weekend."

Toby eyed the back of the truck. "Well, I came out here to see if you needed help carrying anything in, but it looks like they wiped you out. That's awesome." He rocked back on his heels. "So, I'm guessing, now that you finally won Orion, you'll want me to take you out of the dating rotation too, huh? I never expected Tanner and you to drop out so quickly, but I understand."

Damn. Tucker hadn't thought about any of this. He hadn't been thinking of anything but Orion. "I don't know. Probably. I can't imagine going on dates with other people will go over well with Orion. But, hey, Orion gave our card to a BDSM master who does live demos. The guy is pretty hot too. Orion thinks some of these rich people will trip over themselves to have Mister do demonstrations at parties."

Toby's eyebrows rose. "The guy's name is Mister?"

Tucker shrugged. "It's possible it's a pseudonym. He's an author."

Toby seemed to turn inside himself a bit. "It sounds like we need to hire Orion too. That would be a great addition to our team. I can see people wanting that. Scandalous parties are a growing trend. Hopefully, he'll call." His eyes cleared as he focused on Tucker. "I'm going to get mushy for half a second and then leave it alone. I'm really happy for you. Tanner and you. I never thought any of us would have a normal life, but y'all are trying. If we have to shut down the business tomorrow, so you two can have the life you deserve, then that's what we'll do. I just want everyone to have the happiness they deserve."

"Why are you talking about shutting down the business?"

Tucker jumped and spun as Orion appeared behind him—like missing the guy had conjured him. "Hey. I thought you needed a couple of hours."

Orion shrugged, looking as serious as ever. "I changed my mind and headed on over. No one answered at the house. So, I used the GPS tracker I placed on your phone to find you. That's a joke, by the way. I could hear you two talking when I got out of my car."

Tucker snorted. He thought Orion was hilarious. He had literally no deliverance when it came to telling jokes. That's what made him so funny. Before he could say as much, Orion focused on Toby.

"Is there some way I can help with Cubs for Rent? I don't want you to have to close." Orion kept his gaze locked on Toby even as he moved to stand in Tucker's hold. "Did Tucker tell you I gave a guy at the conference a card?"

Toby nodded. "Thanks for that. I hope he calls. With Tanner married and now Tucker being out too, I don't know how to keep things moving forward without help. I can only accept so many dates myself and our staff isn't growing as fast as I hoped."

Orion's forehead furrowed. "Why would Tucker be out?"

"Well, I mean," Toby said, dragging out the words. "You two are together now, finally I might add. It can't be conducive to a good relationship for him to keep accepting dates."

To Tucker's surprise, Orion shrugged. "Well, I mean, it's not real. It's just a job, right? Kind of like going somewhere with a friend... in a way. If I didn't trust him, I wouldn't be here."

Toby blinked. "Wow. I feel like I just met like an actual adult, and now I don't know how to act around you because that's never happened to me before."

Orion shook his head. "You're ridiculous."

"You're a treasure," Toby said back, sounding sincere and proving why Tucker had always been proud to be his brother. Toby glanced around as if he had made himself uncomfortable. Tucker got it. They hadn't been raised to be normal or share feelings. "Well, I guess I need to head out. I plan to stop by the rehabilitation center and check on Loyal."

"Is that your friend who had the bad wreck?"

At Orion's question, Toby met his gaze again. "Yeah. He should get to go home soon. They've been teaching him how to live a normal life in a wheelchair and he's been working on trying to walk again, even if it's just a few steps here and there to make it easier to live alone. He has the heart of a lion."

"And a lifetime ban from the zoo," Tucker said, cutting in.

Orion bit his bottom lip and shook his head, but Tucker could see the smile he tried to hide. Being used to his idiocy, Toby kept talking like nothing happened. Tucker couldn't stop smiling. He loved making Orion laugh, even if it was at him and not with him.

As Orion nodded along while Toby talked about Loyal, Tucker realized something. Orion was the serious adult they didn't know how to be. He went to work every day, made decisions on his own, and took things to heart. Tucker was proud to be with him. Orion's gaze slid his way, catching him staring. He smiled, and that pride doubled. Tucker would give whatever it took to keep him happy. Nothing in his life mattered more.

HE HAD SO MUCH TO DO AROUND HIS PLACE IT wasn't funny, but it was Tucker. It was Tucker and that goddamn question about when Orion's lease ended. That question was under his skin. It was eating his brain. Orion needed to know why. Instead of working up the courage to ask, Orion chose instead to seduce Tucker the instant he had him alone.

As they cleared Tucker's bedroom door, Orion's hands found Tucker's waist. He moved closer, wrapping his arms around Tucker and pressing against his back. Orion inhaled Tucker's scent as he pressed his cheek to Tucker's spine. He had watched Tucker so many times and wanted to hold him just like this. Orion couldn't explain the emotions bursting through him now that he was free to touch Tucker as he pleased.

Tucker stroked his arms. "Are you okay?"

Orion nodded against his back. "You make me happy. I think I should've been saying that more. You've always made me smile and laugh. I go to bed thinking about you and wake up to thoughts of you. I should've been telling you that every day. You deserve that from me."

Tucker turned in his arms. "Your touch burns me alive. I'm toast," he said with a chuckle as Orion rolled his eyes. He lifted Orion's feet from the floor until they were face to face—like Orion was a tiny kid instead of a full-grown man. Tucker's expression was serious despite his bad joke. His gaze was intense as he held Orion's stare. "I love you."

Orion wrapped his legs around Tucker and held on. "I love you too."

Tucker laughed at his antics. The sound swelled Orion's chest. He wasn't the jokester. Tucker did a lot of laughing at him, because of his awkwardness, and inability to do anything Tucker tried to get him to do. It was rare for him to actually pull a laugh from Tucker by playing around.

"You should take off your pants."

Tucker huffed. "Just my pants? Nothing else? I'm starting to think you're only interested in my dick."

"Well, I mean, I plan to take my pants off too. So, we'll be even."

Tucker chuckled. "I guess I finally found something you're willing to do with me that you enjoy."

A smile stretched Orion's lips. "Maybe you should've been throwing different balls at my face."

Tucker roared with laughter.

Orion took a steadying breath. He loved that sound. "Your laughter makes me wish I had a better sense of humor."

To his surprise, Tucker's good humor disappeared. His expression turned serious. "You're the most amazing person I've ever met. I never smiled and meant it before you."

Orion didn't care if Tucker was being truthful. His heart definitely didn't care. That hopeless organ lapped up every word. "Do you plan to take me to bed now?"

Without a word and with Orion wrapped

around his body like a monkey, Tucker headed for the bed. He crawled onto the bed and eased Orion down before settling between his thighs. He held Orion's stare as he lowered his head. Orion's heart pounded so hard his heartbeat thumped in his ears. Tucker's intensity was mesmerizing. He was worth a million possible heart breaks. Tucker was worth all the missed chores and delayed errands. Orion was scared of what he was willing to give up for any amount of time with Tucker.

Tucker's lips brushed Orion's. Orion took a hard breath as Tucker's kiss knocked the air from his lungs. Tucker's hand slid down Orion's body and slipped beneath his ass. He tilted Orion's hips before grinding down on him. Orion gasped around Tucker's tongue. Tucker kissed a path to Orion's neck. Orion sucked air as Tucker's hips rocked. He slowly made love to Orion in their clothes. Orion's feet moved restlessly. He was slightly frustrated. Orion wanted more. His skin was on fire. Tucker held him in place as he kept up the pace, moving against him. If Orion had ever come in his clothes, he couldn't recall the instance. It was about to happen now, and he wasn't sure how he felt about it.

"Oh, fuck. What are you doing to my head?"

Tucker moved back to his lips. "Making you feel

how much I love you," Tucker whispered before deepening their kiss.

Jesus. He felt it. It built in his chest. Orion fought to get closer. His body was wound tight. A whimper filled the air. It took Orion a moment to realize he was the one making the sound. He couldn't stop. "I'm going to come."

"I want it," Tucker growled. "Give it to me."

Orion dug his fingers into Tucker and held on. Reality was slipping away. All Orion knew was the sensation of Tucker moving against him. Orion's breath caught in his throat. He couldn't drag anymore air into his lungs. Everything stopped. Orion's stomach caved. The first spasm hit. A cry burst from Orion. Tucker didn't stop. He dragged every bit of pleasure from Orion until Orion was no more than a puddle of uselessness beneath him.

A chuckle escaped Orion as his current predicament sank in. He was fully clothed with cum filling his underwear and shorts. "I'm a mess."

"I'll clean you up," Tucker said, pushing from the bed.

A hint of disappointment sneaked in at Tucker's willingness to stop when Orion hadn't gotten a chance to make Tucker fly. Then, Tucker turned and met his stare. He looked turned on and in love. The mixture completely wrecked Orion's mind.

"Come and take a shower with me."

Orion practically leapt from the bed and rushed to join Tucker. He had never been more excited to drop to his knees in his life. Tucker had no idea what Orion could and would do for him. He wouldn't stop until Tucker screamed his name and begged for peace. Orion would keep this man happier than he had ever been in his life, because that's exactly how Tucker made him feel.

EIGHT

ORION CHEWED his bottom lip and stared into the dark as Tucker toyed with his fingers. Tucker's hand moved to Orion's hip. His fingertips swiped up and down Orion's bare skin, leaving a trail of goosebumps behind. He should be exhausted. Tucker had definitely done everything in his power to completely drain Orion. But that damn question about his lease wouldn't let him sleep. It grew and grew, pressing on Orion's brain until he thought he might scream. He couldn't take it. "Why did you ask about my lease earlier?" The question burst from Orion with way more intensity than necessary.

Tucker pulled him closer and kissed his neck. "It doesn't matter. I was hoping... it doesn't matter," he repeated, making Orion insane.

"It ends on the fifteenth of next month," Orion said before he could take it back.

He felt Tucker tense. "Are you going to renew?"

Orion shrugged. "I don't know. My landlord doesn't require any specific notice. So," he shrugged again. "I don't know."

Tucker went back to trailing his fingertips up and down Orion's hip. "You could always move in with me. I like having you in my bed."

Orion bit his bottom lip, trying to squelch his happiness before it grew too big. "I suppose I could, if you're really sure you want me here full time." The room spun. Orion found himself on his back with a huge Tucker squashing him to the bed.

"Are you being serious? Are you telling me yes right now?"

Orion blinked at the sudden change. "Yeah, that's what I heard myself say."

Tucker didn't soften. "Don't fuck with me here, Orion. Are you really going to let me keep you?"

He didn't fully understand Tucker's mood. He had been the one to ask, but he sounded like he couldn't believe Orion would agree. "Yeah. I mean, that's typically what yes means, in this case, I suppose. Not that I love you making me sound like

I'm a stray dog or something you're taking in, but I guess I am a stray in a way, so yeah."

A sexy sounding chuckle escaped Tucker. "There's the sexy cranky pants I fell in love with."

A hint of petulance set in. "I'm not cranky. I'm logical and tired a lot."

Tucker kissed Orion's neck, making it hard for him to think straight. "Why are you tired?"

"Um." He chased his thoughts. "I have to get up early every day and work with assholes. It's mentally exhausting."

"You should quit," Tucker said, settling down next to Orion again.

A snort escaped Orion. "I can't quit."

"Of course, you can. You've got me. If you want, you never have to work again." Tucker snapped his fingers. His excitement sounded in his voice. "You could stay home with me and I'll pay you to be my assistant. I'll write. You do the online marketing. Books don't sell themselves, you know."

Orion was grateful for the darkness hiding his eye roll. "I don't know a damn thing about online marketing."

He felt Tucker shrug. "You can learn on the job. Just think about it, okay? I'm not trying to take over your life or anything. It's just that it's my job to make you happy. I love seeing you smile. So, when you're ready, tell that place to fuck off and come home to me. I'll find something for you to do."

Orion was too tired to argue tonight. Plus, he needed to get up early for work. "I'll think about it, sexy." Even to Orion's ears, he sounded like he was falling asleep. He snuggled closer. "I promised myself I would throw everything into this without holding back." Orion's voice slurred. Sleep tugged him deeper, pulling him away from Tucker. His eyes were too heavy to fight now that his questions had been answered. He was finally home.

TUCKER COULDN'T STOP WATCHING ORION sleep. Never in a million years had Tucker believed he would convince Orion to move in with him. He definitely never expected it to be easy. Orion's half-asleep confession about throwing everything into this relationship wouldn't leave Tucker's mind. He had never thought Orion would move in with him, so he didn't know why he had pressed by asking Orion to quit his job too. That would never happen, and he didn't want to take advantage of Orion giving this his all. But still, he hated the idea of Orion working a job he hated. It seemed wrong for Orion to go to work at all when Tucker could give him anything he wanted. From the day they met, he had felt like whatever was his was also Orion's. His home had felt like Orion's. Orion's home had been open to him. They were a pair. A team. He had to find a way to fix this.

Quietly, Tucker rolled and grabbed his phone. He checked the time and then sent off a quick text.

Tucker: *Are you home?*

Toby: *Yep. I'm in the kitchen.*

Tucker: *I'm on my way down. I need to talk to you about something.*

Toby: *Okay. I'll be here.*

With one eye locked on Orion, Tucker slipped from the bed. He didn't want to wake Orion, but he needed to talk to Toby. If Tucker knew nothing else, he knew Toby could help. Toby was the craftiest person Tucker knew. If anyone could convince Orion to walk away from everything for them, it was the brother who always saved him.

THE USUAL SOUND OF ORION'S PHONE, SOUNDING the alarm for him to get up, blared through the room. For a moment, Orion scrambled to find his bedside table before he remembered he was at Tucker's. After three weeks of staying every night with Tucker, Orion should have adjusted somewhat. For the most part, he guessed he had. Except for at odd moments —like now.

Orion hurriedly silenced his phone, hoping not to wake Tucker. As usual, Tucker didn't move. He was the heaviest sleeper Orion had ever seen. Orion smiled at the sight of him sleeping peacefully before slipping from the bed. Orion made his way downstairs. The house was silent. He loved that this place was every bit as peaceful as his home. There was never a TV blaring. It was simply quiet. For someone like him, someone raised with constant noise, nonstop yelling and screaming, the silence was comforting. He understood—from reading Tucker's books—why the triplets didn't have a busy house. They had been raised in the middle of the woods without technology. Not having background noise was normal for them.

Now they lived in a huge gray stone piece of art. It was only two stories, but it was sprawling. More than that, it was in the perfect and most beautiful location. Surrounded by trees and on the edge of Lake Travis, it was secluded and quiet. The guys had the most gorgeous pool Orion had ever seen. It looked like a natural body of water with rocks and a waterfall but was all manmade. Tucker's house was a little slice of Heaven.

As Orion cleared the kitchen door, he found Toby sitting at the kitchen table, staring into space. A mug of coffee was cupped between his hands. Steam rose from the cup. He obviously hadn't been sitting there long, but if he noticed Orion at all, he didn't react. Orion watched him for a moment, hoping not to startle him. It was funny. When he had first met the triplets, he had met Tanner first. Back then, he hadn't been able to tell the triplets apart. Now, he had no trouble distinguishing them. Tanner was the too-serious one. Tucker was the jokester. Toby... he was the caretaker. The nurturer. He worried Orion.

"Are you okay?" Orion kept his voice soft, hoping not to startle him.

Toby blinked, as if coming back to himself. He smiled sweetly. "I'm good. How are you this morning?"

"Good. Is it okay if I have some coffee?"

"Of course. This is your home," Toby said, moving as if to stand.

Orion motioned for him to stay. "It isn't, but I get what you're saying. I've been here enough times to find my way around."

Toby chuckled. "I suppose you have. When will you be moving in permanently?"

Orion concentrated on pouring his coffee to hide his surprise. Toby didn't pull any punches. He was always one to jump right in. "In a couple of weeks," Orion answered honestly, setting the pot aside. He headed to the table to join Toby. "That's when the lease runs out on my house."

Toby nodded. His serious expression never changed. "I'm glad. Tucker always looks like a lost puppy when you're not here. How much do you make working for the city?" Before Orion had time to respond or adjust to the sudden topic change, Toby clarified. "I'm not being nosy or questioning your worth. There's a legitimate reason for my inquiry."

Talking about money didn't bother Orion. He wasn't one to be easily offended. "Sixty-two thousand a year. Why?" he asked as he brought his cup to his lips.

"I'll pay you eighty thousand to work for Cubs for Rent."

Orion froze mid sip. He set his cup aside. "No one wants to date me. I don't think I would be a good candidate for this."

A smile exploded across Toby's face. "I didn't

mean as an escort, but now I'm curious. Why do you think no one would want you for a date?"

Orion shrugged. "I suppose I'm not a typical candidate. Also, I'm awkward. I don't know how to make small talk nor can I flirt. There's no category for me. I'm not muscular and perfectly styled. No one would consider me a bubbly twink." Orion gestured wildly, searching for a way to describe himself. "I don't know. I'm not like Tucker. He's gorgeous and funny. People want to be around him. No one rushes to be near me."

"Tucker does."

Orion snorted. "Yeah, well. He's a weirdo."

The silent laughter in Toby's eyes and his smile was nice to see. "You're exactly what he needs." Toby's smile slipped away. "You do realize, the people who laugh and joke, the ones who always do and say whatever it takes to make other people smile —people like Tucker—are the unhappiest, right? Those are the ones that need other people to laugh, so they know happiness exists, even if they never feel it. They know what real pain and loneliness is like. Those are the ones trying to save everyone else from what they suffer. Tucker needs you." Toby straightened in his chair and blinked, as if coming back to himself. "Besides, you are gorgeous, and anyone would love to have you on their arm, but you have something else I need. You can look at a situation and think outside the box. Creatively. We need that. Plus, I'll need you to go with us to a charity ball tonight. I'll get you a tux later today."

"I'm sorry. What?" Orion wasn't going to a ball. No one was pulling him into that bullshit.

Toby nodded, as if it was already settled. "Tucker and I have clients already. I talked to Mister and he'll join us there. It's the perfect event to introduce him and get people excited for his services. I need you to stick to his side and chat with people. There will be a ton of escorts there. This is one of those events where everyone will want to be seen with the hottest date and will pay any amount to ensure they have it. I want those escorts on our site. If they see Mister getting a ton of interest, then maybe we'll catch their eye." Orion scrambled to find an argument. Toby kept talking, refusing to give him a chance. "Tucker and I need to move into management roles and stop taking clients. When we go to events, it needs to be because we're keeping an eye on our employees and not because we've been hired to be there. We can't do that until we have more escorts at our disposal. So, really, you need to come work for us. After all, when he starts attending all these events as management, you'll want to be there too. You know, so he's not left standing on the sidelines, looking awkward and alone."

Orion wanted to growl. Toby just had to tack on that last bit. He would never want anyone to stand on the sidelines, feeling awkward. That was usually him. "I'll consider your offer."

Toby smiled. "That's all I can ask. You have an appointment at one today to get your tux."

A huff escaped Orion without his permission. The Kodiak brothers were maddening. They never quit until they had their way. Everyone else was just road debris. "I have to work today."

"I know you do. You're working for me."

Orion bit back a growl. "I'm telling you, you'll be sorry. When I get there tonight and no one talks to me, you'll see. I don't fit in anywhere."

"You'll be great. I believe in you."

Orion shook his head. "You're such a pain. Is this how you treat Loyal every day when you go to see him? Do you just make him do whatever you think is best?"

Toby didn't look the least bit guilty. Not that Orion was very good at guilt tripping anyone. Toby shrugged and sipped his coffee. "This is how I treat everyone who needs a kick in the pants to see their worth. You'll get used to it. So, eighty thousand a year... is that what we're shaking on?"

"Jesus," Orion breathed, trying to keep up. He had no idea how he had landed in this mess. One day, a crazy Kodiak brother had chased him through the parking lot of a bar. The next, another brother chased him down the driveway of this house. Now, he was exhausted from all the running and couldn't imagine being anywhere else. These men, they were completely insane. He loved them all so damn much. Tucker was right. This was the family he had chosen. He would do anything to keep them, even if that meant taking eighty grand and putting on a tux. Fuck his life.

NINE

EVERY TIME TUCKER glanced Orion's way, he was smiling and laughing at something Mister said. He was completely focused on the guy. Jealousy roiled in Tucker's gut. The harder he tried not to look their way, the more often his face turned that way. Orion looked gorgeous. He was supposed to be with Tucker. Tucker tried telling himself it wasn't real. They were drumming up business. Putting on a show. Gathering interest in Mister. The thing was, everyone was looking at Orion.

Orion was so fucking beautiful. He was like a tiny sprite with those sexy eyes. The accents on his tux matched those gorgeous eyes to perfection, making them pop. There wasn't a man there who hadn't rushed Orion's way at least once, including the guy paying Tucker to be there. The possessiveness burning through Tucker's veins turned uglier by the minute, especially once the alcohol started flowing. Tucker wasn't much of a drinker, but he hoped the liquor would cool the rage that grew bigger by the minute. The opposite happened.

As Tucker looked on, Mister's hand slid across the small of Orion's back and he leaned close to Orion's ear. Orion nodded and they headed for the door together. Tucker's eye twitched.

"Are you ready to go? It looks like other people are leaving already and we won't be accused of skipping out."

Tucker's gaze swung Kevin's way. The guy hired him more than any other, so Tucker felt twice the pressure to be professional. "Sounds good." He tried for a smile and hoped it wasn't too feral. Mister was about to get his arms ripped off.

As they headed for the door, Kevin moved closer, and motioned Orion's way. "I believe I heard that guy right there works for the same company as you do. Um, the little one with the dark hair."

Tucker thought he might have cracked a back tooth in his bid for restraint. "Yes, but he's in management. He doesn't accept dates." It was the best story Tucker could come up with without killing anyone.

Kevin flashed him a luminous smile. "Actually, I'm a bit relieved to hear that. I don't wish to seem rude, or to impose upon our friendship, but could I trouble you to pass along my card to him? If he's willing, I'd love to take him to dinner. For real. Not as a business arrangement."

Tucker's left eye twitched again. He pressed against it, hoping to make it stop. "He's getting married soon."

"Oh." Kevin's disappointment was palpable.

A hint of guilt sneaked in. "The blond guy with him might be interested. He's also not offering dates as part of his services."

Kevin shook his head. "No, thank you. I actually know him very well. He's not a good person."

Shit. Orion was leaving with him and there was nothing Tucker could do without harming their business. He scrambled for a way to go to Orion. "Should I be worried about Orion? I mean, should I warn him about something specific or be concerned about his safety?"

"Orion," Kevin repeated with a smile. "That's a fitting name. I don't think he's in any physical danger. Haven is more of a serial seducer than anything else."

The rage was back. Tucker would destroy Mister if he touched Orion. They ended up standing at Mister and Orion's back, waiting their turn for the valet to bring Kevin's car. Orion glanced over his shoulder and winked. Tucker's heart twisted in his chest. Orion belonged to him.

Kevin touched Orion's shoulder, bringing his gaze back his way. "Excuse me. Would you like a ride home?" His gaze slid Mister's way before returning to Orion. "We would see you home safely," he said, leaving no doubt he didn't think Mister would leave Orion at his door untouched.

Orion took Mister's arm. "No, thank you. I have a ride."

Tucker's mood darkened, turning pitch black. He could have ridden home with Kevin and Tucker, leaving Mister free to go home. He was openly choosing to go with Mister instead. Tucker seethed as he watched Orion leave with another man. It didn't matter to his heart that it was work related. One of his black moods was brewing. All the way to the house, he stewed. Orion was supposed to move in with him in less than two weeks. They were real. This was permanent. Mister didn't get to waltz in with his practiced smiles, whips, and chains and steal what belonged to Tucker.

Still, as Kevin dropped him at his door, Tucker managed a smile and small talk. He thanked the man for a nice evening. Then, he went inside with murder on his mind. Orion wasn't there. He headed back toward the door, texting Orion along the way.

Tucker: *Where are you?*

Orion: *Home.*

The eye twitch was back.

Tucker: *No, you're not. I'm home and you're not here.*

Orion: *My home. Not yours.*

Tucker: *This is our home.*

Orion: *Not for two more weeks. For now, I still live here. This is where all my things are.*

Tucker: *Is one of those things Mister?*

Orion: *He's here too, if that's what you're asking.*

Tucker would fucking kill him. He wasn't playing. Since he had been drinking—like a dumbass —he couldn't drive. He was mad at everyone, including himself. His phone buzzed again.

Orion: *Why do I get the feeling you're mad at me?*

He didn't bother answering. After all, there weren't any men at his house. Tucker had come home alone. He wasn't the one entertaining someone else. It seemed he was the only one who recognized this was just a job, after all. Toby walked through the door, smiling brightly.

"Hey, bro. Things went great tonight. Orion was amazing."

Tucker pried his back teeth apart. "Yep. Amazing. Can you give me a lift to his place? I've been drinking."

Toby eyed him, as if trying to decipher his tone. Tucker flashed him a smile, hiding his rage. He knew his brother. If Toby knew what was in his head, he would try to save Tucker from himself by refusing to help. After a moment, he shrugged. "Sure. I've got nothing else going on. Did you want to change or anything?"

No time. Tucker was at stroke level fury. "Nope. I have clothes there."

"All right," Toby said, opening the door he had just closed behind him. "After you."

"Thank you."

Toby smiled—like all was right with the world. "Of course. You know I'm a sucker for love."

Somehow, Tucker managed a chuckle. He worried it sounded every bit as evil as he felt. Tucker didn't recall a second of the drive to Orion's house. His phone buzzed several times, but he was too angry to see clearly. Mister's classic Mustang still sat in Orion's driveway, proving he was a goddamn idiot.

"Hey, it looks like Mister got Orion home safely."

"Sure," Tucker said, jumping from the truck. "Thanks for the ride." He slammed the door behind him without waiting to hear Toby's response.

Toby climbed from the still running truck. "Hold up, Tucker. What's going on? Is everything okay?"

Tucker didn't slow. He stormed the back door that opened into Orion's kitchen. Thankfully, it was unlocked. Tucker wasn't sure he wouldn't have kicked it in if it hadn't been, even though he knew where Orion kept his spare key. Laughter filled the kitchen. He barely took in the room with one sweeping glance. It was enough to glean that they were having a grand time. Mister sat at Orion's tiny kitchen table while Orion sat on the kitchen counter. Orion wore sweat shorts and a t-shirt, proving he had been undressed in the same house as Mister. That was enough for him.

"Hey, baby. Why haven't you been answering my texts? You won't believe—"

Tucker charged Mister, fully intent on killing him. Mister's eyes widened as he scrambled from the chair and Orion slid in between them faster than he had ever seen Orion move. Too fast, in fact. Tucker's forward momentum completely bowled him over. Everything inside Tucker froze as Orion hovered in the air for half a second before he went sprawling. It was like time slowed. Everything happened too fast for him to stop it and too slowly for him to miss a single detail. He swore he felt the thud of Orion's head bouncing off the hard kitchen floor. The air caught and stuck in his throat.

"What the fuck are you doing?" Toby's angry yell cut through the air behind him before he shoved Tucker aside.

Tucker hit his knees. Everything else stopped mattering the instant he harmed Orion. He would fucking die before ever hurting Orion, but he had. In that moment, he was his father. Words crowded his throat as he reached for Orion. He had no clue what he said. Tucker tried apologizing and explaining at the same time, but it came out a babbled mess. Toby pushed his hands away before he could touch Orion.

As Tucker looked on, Toby cupped Orion's face. "Orion. Talk to me. Are you okay?"

Mister joined in, blocking Tucker's view. He couldn't see anything. Everything was a blur. In that moment, Tucker was convinced Orion was dead. Even if he hadn't killed him, he had definitely murdered their love. He was his father, butchering everything beautiful he touched. It should be him. He was better off dead. Tucker should have died out in those woods with his father—put down like the rabid animal he was.

With his back pressed to the kitchen cabinet, Tucker sat. He saw nothing. Pain and horrible memories owned him. Orion was the one good thing in his life. Everything was gone now. People moved around him. Tucker heard wheezing—like a severe asthma attack. Nothing made sense. His eyes wouldn't work. He wanted to check on Orion and keep him safe. The room spun. Something tapped his cheek.

"Breathe, idiot."

Tucker tried to focus at the words. It sounded like Orion's voice. He blinked. Something warm trailed down his face.

"Goddamn it, Tucker. Take a breath."

Tucker sucked air. His vision cleared. Orion was inches from his face. The room slowly came into focus. Orion sat back on his ass—hard. He had an ice pack held to the back of his head.

"Could everyone leave, please?"

"Orion," Mister said, obviously gearing up to argue. It couldn't have been more obvious he didn't think Orion should be alone with Tucker.

Tucker was still too frozen with shame, fear, and guilt to move.

Orion just sounded tired as he cut off whatever Mister had been about to say. "I'll be fine. It's late. Everyone should get home."

"If you're sure..."

Toby slapped Mister across the back and steered him toward the door. "Orion has things under control. I trust him. He wouldn't be kicking us out if he didn't feel safe here."

Orion didn't watch them go. His gaze never wavered from Tucker. The moment the door closed behind them, Orion took a deep breath. His chest expanded and his shoulders fell. "Are you okay?"

Tucker swallowed. His throat hurt. It took a moment, but he found his voice. "I should be the one asking you that."

Orion dropped his arm and cradled the ice pack between his hands in his lap. "Do you want to tell me what just happened?"

"I don't know."

Orion's brow furrowed. "You don't know what happened or you don't know if you want to tell me?"

Tucker blinked. His mind still wasn't clear. Everything felt like it was on fire. He thought maybe it was the sensation of his life burning to the ground.

Orion scooted closer and took Tucker's wrist, grounding him with his touch. Tucker's fingers closed around Orion's wrist too. They held on to each other. Tucker swallowed again. "I'm scared."

Orion's expression never faltered. He looked calm. Of course, Orion was always calm. "You can talk to me, baby."

"I hurt you."

"You didn't mean to. That doesn't mean you're off the hook, but you need to talk to me. That wasn't you who just burst through my kitchen door."

Tucker shook his head. "That was my dad. His temper. His jealousy. Everyone was flirting with you and begging for your attention. Instead of being proud—like you deserve, I was angry. Then, Kevin wanted me to give you his number and started saying you weren't safe with Mister. I don't know what happened. One minute, I was there. The next, I was my dad. I couldn't let Mister touch you."

"Can I tell you what you should have done?"

As much as Tucker wanted to smile at Orion's serious tone, he didn't think he would ever smile again. "Please?"

"Check your phone."

Tucker used his free hand to dig his phone from his shirt pocket. He opened his missed texts.

Orion: *I'm changed, have a huge bag packed, and I'm trying to get Mister out of here so I can come to you.*

Orion: *He's still talking, but I'm closer to the door. I packed enough stuff that I don't have to come back here until next weekend. If you want, we can start moving me in then. That way, you don't have to worry about where I call home.*

Orion: *Actually, I have something else I want to talk to you about. I decided tonight that I'm a chicken shit and should have talked to you sooner. Don't go to sleep before I get there.*

If Tucker hadn't already felt like the worst person on the planet, now his pain was double. While he had been seething, Orion had been trying his damnedest to get to him.

He dropped his phone and banged his head against the cabinet behind him.

Orion swiped his thumb back and forth across his wrist, openly trying to soothe him. "Do you know why I fell in love with you?"

Tucker's throat swelled. He tried to swallow past it. Tears spilled from his lashes with no control on his part. "No." Even to his ears, Tucker sounded broken. "You shouldn't have."

"I fell in love with this part of you first." Tucker

dropped his chin and met Orion's stare at the claim. He looked as steady as ever. His otherworldly eyes were clear as he waited for Tucker's attention. When he had it, Orion continued. "I fell in love with this unabashedly emotional side of you. You laugh, yell, cry, and love without an ounce of embarrassment. It's all passion driven. If you give a fuck what anyone thinks about how you embrace everything you feel, you don't show it. For someone who went completely unnoticed through life, the intense way that you love me is irresistible. I know you didn't mean to hurt me, but do *you* know it?"

More tears fell. He had never hurt worse in his life and that was saying a lot. "I would rather die than hurt you."

Orion nodded, as if Tucker said exactly what he had expected. "You're not your father."

He didn't deserve Orion.

Orion didn't stop there. "Kevin is Mister's ex. They had an extremely nasty break up. I imagine he said a lot of unnecessary things to you about Mister, but do you know what? None of that has anything to do with us. You will talk to me from now on before getting to this point, understood? I know we have shitty pasts that have damaged us in our own ways, but no matter what it is or when it is, even if you have to walk away from a paying client to come to me, you will talk to me."

"I'm not ever taking another job. I can't. You're the only one for me. I can't let anything come between us. Life is too hard without you."

Orion took a deep breath. He looked sad but he didn't argue. "You should probably apologize to Mister."

"I will."

"Do you ever plan to tell me you love me?"

Tucker fell forward. He couldn't stop it from happening. His head landed in Orion's lap as he rolled onto his side. In a fetal position, he snuggled as close as he could get to Orion, seeking the only comfort he had ever had in this world. "I love you. I'm so, so sorry."

Orion ran his fingers through Tucker's hair. "I know, baby."

Tucker was half a second away from rocking himself in the corner. "Does your head hurt? I'm a terrible person. You shouldn't love me."

"Shush," Orion said, scratching his scalp. "You have shown your love for me way more times than not. I know you. I know your heart. You will take this night to heart and never stop trying to fix it. That's the best anyone can hope for, because no one is perfect. Plus, you're the one for me. I can't imagine my life without you being my constant hurricane. I'm very much in love with you, Tucker Jonas. Your heart is beyond beautiful."

It wasn't, but Tucker would do whatever it took to live up to Orion's opinion. He still felt sick. In fact, he expected this hollow pit in his gut would be permanent. But Orion still loved him. That was the only thing holding him together. Tucker would cling to that.

Orion's insides shook. The way Tucker had melted down was the most terrifying thing he had seen in a long time. The thing was, it was also reassuring on a level Orion had never experienced. Tucker would never hurt him or let anyone else harm him. He would never break Orion's heart or abandon him. If only the idea of harming Orion broke Tucker down like this, Orion had nothing to fear. What terrified Orion the most was Tucker's pain. He would never let any harm come to Tucker—mental or physical. Orion couldn't undo the past, but he could build them a beautiful future, and he would.

He lightly scratched Tucker's scalp. "Are you falling asleep on me?"

Tucker shook his head. "What did you want to talk to me about? Your text said you had something to say."

He did, but now felt like a horrible time. "This feels like a bad time. You don't love yourself right now."

Tucker pressed his face to Orion's stomach. Orion could feel his hot tears through his shirt. He had never seen Tucker hurting like this. It was horrible. He never wanted to see it again. Maybe it wasn't such a bad time after all. It was possible he could fix it.

"Just don't laugh at me, and I'll say what I need to say, okay? I know I'm a hedgehog." He felt Tucker press his face harder against his stomach, making Orion wonder if he was trying not to laugh. "I said not to laugh at me."

"I'm not," Tucker said, his voice muffled against Orion's skin.

Mollified, Orion continued. "I know that I'm prickly and I make people work to get close to me. You know why I am the way I am. There's no need for me to rehash it. I hate noise, yet you're the loudest person I know and I can't live without you. You have no idea how many times I've mused over that one. I think it's because—to me—you're not busy noise. You're more like music." He felt Tucker relax, so he kept talking. "Sometimes you're soothing and other times you lift my mood." Orion smiled and ran his fingers through Tucker's hair. "Sometimes you match my rage. No matter what, we fit. Tonight, some guy offered me an eye-popping amount of money to go home with him. That's why I stayed glued to Mister, because I didn't feel safe, and you had a client. Obviously, I wasn't the least bit tempted to accept that guy's offer. But do you know how I responded?"

Tucker rolled onto his back and met Orion's stare. He looked a complete mess. "Did you tell him you're already married and should back the fuck off?"

A smile exploded across Orion's face. He couldn't help it. "Yes. That's exactly what I said, and you know what? I realized as I said the words that it felt real. It didn't feel like a lie, and that's when I knew I had to try to make it as real as it felt. So, would you like to get hitched?"

Tucker didn't answer right away, and Orion almost took it back. "When Kevin asked me to pass his number along, I told him you were engaged."

Tucker's admission startled a chuckle from Orion. They were a pair. Tucker's gaze locked on to Orion with so much intensity the sound died on his lips. He shook his head. His voice came out sounding strained. "It didn't feel like a lie." Tucker visibly swallowed. "It felt like he was trying to put his foot in my marriage, and I couldn't let him. I don't want it to be a lie."

Orion's chest swelled with happiness and pride. "Then we'll make it real."

Tucker took his hand and brought it to his mouth. "We will," he whispered against Orion's skin. "Will you take my last name?" Tucker asked, sounding excited and showing the first sign of life.

Orion jumped on the chance to lighten the mood. "I think I kind of have to."

Tucker's forehead furrowed. "Why would you have to?"

"Because you're a Kodiak. Life without you would be un-bear-able."

The sound that left Tucker was somewhere between a snort and laugh, but his eyes finally danced with happiness. "Jesus. I love you."

Orion chuckled. "I've been saving that one for a rainy day. I love you too, baby. Do you think you'll be okay now? My head is killing me, and I could really use some ibuprofen."

Tucker immediately rolled into a sitting position in a sexy use of ab strength that made Orion's mouth water. "Shit. I'm still on the floor, melting down, while you're the one who's hurt. Come on, baby. I'll take care of you." He swept Orion from the floor and into his arms. Tucker was so strong and sexy. It never stopped blowing Orion away that Tucker not only wanted Orion, but he let himself be vulnerable for Orion. Orion had gone into this thing, knowing Tucker had issues. He wouldn't give up on him over one breakdown. There was no one better in his eyes.

Tucker carried Orion to bed and tucked him in. "Give me a minute. I'll grab you a bottle of water and something for the pain."

Orion nodded. His head was sore—like a huge knot was growing. As he watched, Tucker peeled off his jacket and shirt before tossing aside his belt. Suddenly, Orion's blankets felt like too much. Heat spread beneath them. Tucker left the room, leaving him disappointed. Thankfully, he wasn't gone long. With Orion's giant duffel bag looped over his shoulder, a bottle of water in one hand and pills in the other, Tucker was back in no time. He dumped Orion's bag in a chair by the bedroom door before joining Orion on the bed. Tucker opened his water for him and dug out two pills. He looked entirely too serious for Orion's taste.

"I brought your bag, in case you need anything in it before bed."

Orion swallowed his pills and shook his head. "All I need is you."

Tucker nodded. "I'll sleep on top of the covers, so you don't have to worry about me bothering you," he said, settling into the spot next to Orion on his side. "I'll keep an eye on you for any signs of a concussion."

A snort escaped Orion before he could call it back. He tossed the covers aside. "Okay. That's enough of that. I'm not a weakling." To emphasize his point, Orion tumbled Tucker onto his back. "I'm the only one who decides what I can handle and what I can't. No way did I spend the night watching you from across the room, and convince you to marry me, to let you sleep on top of the covers. I've never had a headache that damn bad in my life." Tucker didn't fight him but nor did he help. He stayed completely still as Orion kissed his neck. Orion moved to his collarbone and then his nipple. Tucker stirred beneath him. Orion fought a smile as Tucker released a reluctant sounding moan. After one last flick of his tongue across Tucker's nipple, Orion slipped farther down the bed. He counted Tucker's ribs with his tongue as he slithered lower. Orion set Tucker's erection free as he went, but he didn't touch it. Instead, he licked around Tucker's cock, ensuring he stayed close enough to drive Tucker insane. It was punishment for thinking to sleep above the covers when Orion deserved more.

Orion felt Tucker's muscles tense. That was all the warning he got before he found himself on his back, staring at the ceiling with his dick in Tucker's mouth. Orion's eyes rolled back in his head. Tucker wasn't teasing. He was set to steal Orion's soul. Tucker stopped long enough to bare the bottom half of Orion's body and then he was back. Orion was a panting and babbling mess. He didn't understand what happened anytime he was in a sexual situation with Tucker, but Orion always transformed into a confident and dominant version of himself that he didn't recognize. He grabbed Tucker's hair and hung on. Orion's hips rolled as he took what he wanted from Tucker's mouth. Tucker didn't merely accept Orion's punishment. He reveled in it. Saliva ran down Orion's cock as he slammed against the back of Tucker's throat. Tucker took every ounce of the abuse.

"That's it, sexy. Suck me. Oh, god. Yes. Like that."

Tucker used his saliva coated fingers to fuck Orion's ass. He pumped in and out before curling upward and massaging. Orion couldn't look away. He stared down the length of his body at the love of his life on his dick. The sight was erotic as hell. Tucker's shoulders moved in a way that hypnotized Orion. He was beautiful. Even as pressure built, pounding against his crown, Orion didn't look away. He couldn't. A mewling cry left him. His entire body tensed. He was right on the edge. In a flash of movement, Tucker flew upward and claimed his mouth swallowing his cry of denial. His cock filled Orion's ass at the same time as his tongue filled Orion's mouth. He slammed forward, hitting just the right spot. Orion exploded into oblivion. A loud cry vibrated around their entwined tongues. Orion whimpered as he coated their skin in cum. Tucker's hips rocked, riding him through his orgasm, and making him see stars. His body gave out as the waves died away. He felt his muscles melt to mush—like Tucker had stolen everything from him.

Tucker's lips skimmed his jaw. He could feel Tucker's cock twitching inside him, as he pumped Orion full of cum in a silent orgasm. Orion stroked his hair and let him have his peace. Tears stung the backs of his eyes. He loved Tucker. The full impact of the night washed over him. Tucker's past was black. It was one thing to read about it in a book marked as fictional. Knowing those nightmare stories were true, and seeing firsthand the damage left behind, that was something different. All three of the Kodiak brothers had been through intense counseling. Orion had known that before he had really known why. None of that knowledge had prepared him for witnessing Tucker's pain as it overtook him, making him someone else. His heart hurt. He couldn't ever let Tucker feel this way again.

Orion grabbed Tucker's face and forced the man to hold his stare. "I love you. You never have to worry about us. Not ever. You are my whole world. No one comes before you. I swear that you'll be safe and happy for the rest of your life with me."

Tucker's eyes filled with tears. He kissed Orion, making Orion wonder if it was sealing a vow or hiding his reaction. Either way, he would take it. Orion believed in Tucker in a way he had never believed in anyone. Tucker was right about them. They were the next best thing to Heaven.

TEN

QUITE A FEW PIECES of Orion's furniture had to be donated, since they were no longer needed. The rest of his large pieces were getting delivered by a moving company, but Orion didn't trust anyone touching his books. Orion had forgotten how much he hated moving until after he had made his hundredth trip up the stairs. While Tucker's house had an elevator, it was farther away from Tucker's bedroom than taking the staircase. Orion chose to carry boxes up the stairs over carrying them all the way to the other end of their humongous house and back after the elevator carried him to the second floor.

Bent at the waist, Orion rubbed his left ankle. He was pretty sure it would never be the same after an unfortunate turn on the stairs. "Jesus. How many boxes are left in the truck? I think I seriously underestimated my ability to handle this much physical labor. At this rate, I won't be able to climb the stairs to go to bed tonight."

"I think there are still like ten boxes," Tucker called from inside the house.

"I'd offer to give you a ride on my lap, but I don't think my chair will make it up the stairs."

Orion sprang upright and spun at the softly spoken words behind him. His eyes landed on the most beautiful man Orion had ever seen in his life. He looked like a model. His lips were full, and his eyes were a gorgeous bluish green—like the water in Jamaica. The guy's blond hair was shaggy with the perfect amount of curl. He stole Orion's voice. Orion would never choose anyone over Tucker. Tucker was his whole world. But this guy literally stunned Orion speechless with his beauty.

Toby chuckled as he pushed the guy's wheelchair closer to the bottom of the porch stairs. "I forgot to warn you about Orion. He's shy."

That wasn't true, and it also wasn't why Orion hadn't responded, but he appreciated the rescue. Orion waved—like an idiot. "Hi."

After Toby pushed the chair as close to the stairs'

handrail as possible, the guy used the rail to pull himself into a standing position. Toby rushed the chair up the stairs and onto the porch, before returning to help the guy climb the stairs and back to his chair. Orion was impressed. Toby had done most of the work, but he had also done a hell of a job making it look like he hadn't.

Tucker stepped outside, smiling. "Well, look at you, Loyal. You're getting around much better than the last time I saw you. I imagine you'll be running marathons in no time."

Loyal winked as he settled back into the wheelchair. "I'm working on it. So, this is the guy you've been talking about nonstop for months. You're right. He is incredibly sexy."

Orion blushed.

Tucker smiled, looking proud. "Yep, this is my fiancé, Orion. Orion, this is Loyal. We all used to play softball together."

Orion smiled, finding his voice. "It's nice to meet you. Toby talks about you a lot. It feels like I already know you."

To Orion's surprise, Toby blushed while Loyal looked a tad bit uncomfortable. Orion was transfixed. He had never seen Toby blush. Orion hadn't known it was possible.

Tucker's arms encircled Orion's waist. He towed Orion against his chest and set his chin on Orion's head. "Are you coming to our wedding?"

"Oh, absolutely," Loyal said, sounding bright. "I got the invitation the other day. You two are adorable. I'm happy for you. Do you have plans for a honeymoon?"

"Aspen," Orion answered for them. "We want to go play in the snow."

Tucker kissed the top of his head. "Yeah. I wanted to take him to the moon, but I hear that place has no atmosphere."

Toby and Loyal groaned. Orion couldn't stop smiling. He could practically feel Tucker's happiness vibrating from him like a physical thing. That was everything to Orion.

"Well, are you ready?" Toby asked Loyal, taking the brakes off Loyal's wheelchair.

"Yep." He waved at them. "I'll catch you later. Toby is taking me out on the lake today. I'm beyond ready for some fresh air."

Orion nodded. "Have fun. We have to get back to dragging boxes up the stairs."

"Good luck," Loyal said over his shoulder as the pair headed inside.

Orion waited until they were gone to speak.

"That was interesting. Are they dating?"

"Oh, boy," Tucker said, dragging out the words. "Well, there's some history there. I'll tell you all about it later." He kissed Orion's neck, making goosebumps rise on his skin. "Right now," he said, speaking against Orion's throat. "We should get back to those boxes in the back of my truck. Or... you could trust me to hire someone to handle it and I could carry you up the stairs. I could make us a hot bubble bath with the jacuzzi jets going. You could sit in my lap and I can rub your back... or any place you'd like me to massage. What do you say?"

Temptation crippled Orion. He loved his books and didn't want any of them damaged, but he loved Tucker more.

"Okay, I—"

Tucker snatched him off his feet before he could finish his thoughts. That was fine. Orion held onto Tucker's neck as he ascended the stairs. He couldn't stop smiling or staring at Tucker's gorgeous face. This man was the rest of his life. They had something better than any story. It was real.

KEEP AN EYE OUT FOR THE NEXT BOOK IN THE series, *Always Loyal*.

ABOUT THE AUTHOR

Charity Parkerson is an award winning and multi-published author with several companies. Born with no filter from her brain to her mouth, she decided to take this odd quirk and insert it in her characters.

*Eight-time Readers' Favorite Award Winner
  *2015 Passionate Plume Award Finalist
  *2013 Reviewers' Choice Award Winner
  *2012 ARRA Finalist for Favorite Paranormal Romance
  *Five-time winner of The Mistress of the Darkpath

Connect with her online:

--Join   my   street   team: facebook.com/TeamCharityParkerson
  --Website: charityparkerson.com
  --Facebook: facebook.com/authorCharityParkerson

facebook.com/TheMenofSin

--Twitter: twitter.com/CharityParkerso